The Oasis of Filth

My Chronicle of the RL2013 Outbreak

A Novel

Part Two

The Hopeless Pastures

Keith Soares

Bufflegoat Books

Second print edition 2.0, March 2014
ISBN 978-0-9899483-4-0

Original publication date November 28, 2013

Many thanks to Chris for his tremendous contributions while editing this book. Additional thanks to Layla, Jeff Yeatman, Bill Setzer, Scott Blum, and Jim Peterson. And a big thank you to Emily Savage for her medical insight.

Edited by Christopher Durso

1

I reeled. The shock of pain and of seeing my skin torn open. The frayed wound began to spout blood, crimson red shining in the warm yellow light. Tilting my head up, I squeezed my eyes against the blazing sun. Blood dripped down, touching the multicolored band at my wrist, and I thought of her, not bringing her name to mind for fear of making it... real. I looked away as I reached for the raw wound.

I thought of her.

Her face, smiling through tears the day we arrived at The Oasis, rose before my squinting eyes, a phantom in the sparkling sunshine.

I closed my eyes, blocking it out. But my other senses betrayed me. Her sound was gone, her touch was gone, her smell was gone.

She was gone.

The blood. My blood. Her blood, flowing. I squinted in the sunlight, embracing the pain. This little pain. This little blood. This comparative nothing.

I waved my injured hand and grimaced. "Sonofa—," I muttered, grasping my bleeding left thumb. The blue crab fell to the dock, skittered sideways, and plopped back into the safety of the water. I looked down at my early-summer harvest of crabs in the boxy wire trap; not bad. In fact, compared to before the outbreak, it was pretty damn good. The crab population must have thought that the lack of humans was about the best thing to ever happen to them.

I considered the trap, wriggling with crabs of various sizes, and figured I'd better wrap up my thumb before picking out any of the others. I had chosen the first because it was the biggest, and paid the price of a snipped-off thumb tip. The others weren't going anywhere, so I lowered the basket back into the water beside the dock and trudged up to the small, single-story waterfront home I had adopted. For a moment I thought of the crabs in the trap, how they walked themselves in but had no idea how to walk out. Like we all had, to our own deadly trap.

Stepping off the small dock and into the long, untended grass, I looked toward the house, seeing it illuminated in the afternoon's warm sunshine. Some of the dry wood siding hung crookedly, there were long rips in the mesh screens of the porch, the screen door had fallen onto the ground beside the steps, and the roof was littered with pine needles and other debris. The better to make it look empty, I figured.

It had taken a long time to find a spot that would avoid notice. For a while, I wasn't even looking, I didn't care. I just wandered. I'd sleep on the ground when I was tired, not concerned about passing zombies. To me, it no longer mattered if I lived or died. I walked on with no destination, nothing but numbness. For no reason at all, I headed south again, this time following the river, then crossed what was left of the old Wilson Bridge into Maryland. There, simply because it was the direction the bridge faced, I turned east. When the bridge ended, I didn't follow the curving Beltway but instead left the highway and broke out east. It was days meandering before I reached the Chesapeake. The idea came to me to just *stop* there. To give up. I turned my head left and spied the long metal arcs of the Bay Bridge. Like a zombie myself, my feet simply started going in that direction. Maybe it was because the western shore had too many memories.

In time, I reached the metal feet of the long, sweeping bridge, stepped over some unguarded barricades, and began to walk the length of the southernmost span. I considered the emptiness stretching before me, feeling it appropriate for the emptiness inside me. I vaguely considered that the military must have cleared away all the cars to keep the bridge open for their needs. The military. That thought alone made me stop walking. I stood there, alone in the middle of the huge span crossing the bay, and looked at my hands, clenching them into fists. Unclenching. Clenching. The only sounds were the wind, waves and a few lonely birds. There was no one to hear, and even if there were, I didn't care. I wailed incomprehensible noises out to the sky, my body shuddering.

Finally exhausted, I gasped to refill my lungs. I looked down toward the low rail along the side of the bridge, considered the great drop to the water below, and envisioned myself there, falling to freedom. But my feet started moving again, seemingly detached from my brain or my heart.

Reaching the Eastern Shore, I turned and looked back. Unlike when I left DC those months ago, this time I did think about this last moment. I thought I would never come this way again. In fact, I hoped that was true. I wanted nothing to do with DC, or *humanity*, ever again. Looking back toward the west, I saw thick undulating clouds rolling, all shades of grey. Winter was coming. I took a drink of water, what remained, and walked on. On the far side of the bridge, cars were strewn like flotsam on the ocean, turned every direction, crushed into one another. An attempt at a great mass exodus had occurred here. Not a soul remained now. I had to leave the highway at times to make any progress through the wreckage, continuing on for days. The sheer number of cars trying to head west, piled up together and yet *empty* was mind-boggling.

Some nights I stayed in houses. Breaking in wasn't hard; most had been left open and abandoned. I found out that anything remotely near the highway had been thoroughly picked over, with nothing left to use. So I went deeper, using the highway, Route 50, as a branching-off point. I stumbled onto homes filled with scared, threatening families… people who had somehow made a life out here hunting and growing for themselves and didn't want company. I hardly noticed their confused looks when their threats of guns barely registered with me, but knew they felt relief when I moved on, leaving them in their version of peace. For days I followed Route 50, as the temperature dropped and the weather threatened.

I holed up in Easton, Maryland, for most of the winter, sleeping in abandoned strip-mall stores and houses. It was a desolate place. I had found a backpack and kept it stocked as best I could with dry foods, some canned goods. The winter was cold and snow was frequent, so travel became more difficult, as did finding food. When the snow would let up, I'd move a bit farther south. One old supermarket looked promising, a place to find a couple of cans to replenish my stock, but inside was a shantytown of dirty, tired souls, huddled together in countless little makeshift rooms. The people there were shell-shocked, hollow. They seemed to be a transient bunch, everyone there for just a day or two before moving on, making my appearance nothing unusual. The kids were the worst; they wore a kind of blank expression, like life had boiled down to the simplicity of *What am I going to do now?* mixed with the apathy of having asked yourself that question far too many times. As I walked among the rows of empty shelves and crowded hovels, amid the smell of too many people on top of each other, a commotion broke out in the back of the store. Some people raced to see what was happening; others were beyond caring. I suppose I fell in the second category, and that's probably why my presence didn't raise any interest; my hollow eyes simply mirrored their own. At the end of one aisle, I could see what was happening. Someone, a young girl, was turning. I figured she probably wouldn't be the only one to do so that night, so I made my way out.

Just as the weather began improving, my food supply was gone. I collected snow to melt for water, but I went without eating for days. One night, I sat staring out the front window of the small appliance store where I was sleeping, and felt pain all over. It was a profound physical weakness, like my body had finally caught up to my mind and decided this was the end. I contemplated the uselessness of it all and faded into a last sleep.

In the morning I awoke, hungry but alive, continuing this life of nothingness. Fate wasn't done with me yet. I found a small stash of canned food tucked inside a cabinet in the store, and ate ravenously. Still with no goal, I plodded farther south that day.

Just after Cambridge, the main road turned west and I turned east. Here, the density changed. Fewer homes, more open land. Approaching one abandoned house, I heard a shot ring out, a *whoosh* of air whipping past me. I stopped and looked up to find a man pointing a long rifle from an upstairs window. I turned and walked off.

Spring was approaching finally. One day, as I was dragging myself over the brown pine-needle-covered floor of some woodland miles from any highway, I spied something just barely peeking over the treetops, turning slowly. Coming closer, I saw a well-concealed wind turbine, the kind for generating electricity. I was suspicious of another warning shot, but slipping out of the woods, I found a low nondescript house that seemed truly abandoned. To one side of the house, past what appeared to be the cap of a water well, stood a small clearing for growing crops; on the opposite was the riprapped edge of the Chesapeake Bay. A thin pier struck out into the choppy water, with no boat in sight. Perhaps these people had given up their home and set sail for the western shore and the promise of safety in DC. Maybe they heard the bridge was blocked and the water was their only escape. Who knew?

Figuring there was a good chance that something or someone was still in the house, I explored it gingerly, room to room, thinking every creaking board could be sealing my fate. Finally, when I realized it was completely empty, I stood in the kitchen. Thinking of the spinning turbine outside, I flicked the light switch; nothing. I went to the sink and tried the faucet; also nothing. But I was exhausted and figured the house would make as good a place to die as any other. I stayed.

The next day, I decided to check on the turbine, an exceptionally delicate and dangerous process because I had no way to stop the blades from spinning, but I had to climb up and inspect the head unit anyway. The wind was light, but the blades still turned. I assumed it would be hopeless given what little I knew about electrical systems, but as soon as I opened up the head I saw the issue. The main gear, spinning around and around slowly, belying the danger one wrong move meant, was disconnected from the gear on the generator. Otherwise nothing looked out of sorts, so I figured it might have been built to detach in high winds or out of some other safety consideration. Carefully reaching my hand in, I tried spinning the smaller generator gear manually. It barely moved.

With the promise of electricity so close, the last thing I wanted to do was force things together and break them, so I climbed down and looked for something to help. I found oil in a small shed, and after a while of working it in, the generator gear turned comfortably. As I stood on the ladder rungs, bored from the repetition of oiling the gear but always watching the large blades spinning just a foot away, I saw a lever. A red and yellow sticker had been attached to it long ago, but now only tatters of color remained. I tried it.

The main gear extended on its shaft and caught with the smaller gear on the generator, now turning together as a unit. Despite my precarious location, I clapped my hands in triumph.

Back inside the house, though, nothing worked. I noticed a small metal out-building that housed a bank of batteries and cleaned them of debris and corrosion. I figured I had done enough for one day, and ate some of my last food stocks while sitting on the pier.

The next morning, with the sun not yet up and the woods outside just beginning to lighten, I walked into the kitchen. Incomprehensibly, I heard a low *hum*. My eyes widened, looking toward the refrigerator. Was it... *on?* I went to the light switch by the door. Expecting failure, I reached for it. Flicking up, I was blinded by electric lights. In shock, I quickly flicked them off again, peering out the kitchen window to see if anyone had taken notice. I scurried through the house looking out every window as if an attack was imminent. But as the sun slowly rose, nothing returned my gaze but the bay on one side and the surrounding pines on the other.

That night, I conducted an experiment, one that I repeated many nights. I flicked on one of the lights, still amazed by the power generated from the wind turbine, and stealthily went outside. Ducking into the woods, I made a long, slow circle around the house, gauging how the light travelled. The densely growing pines worked like curtains, blocking the light from passing too far from the house. Over the next few nights, I increased the number of lights and used the house's own shades to diminish the amount of brightness pouring into the woods. After about a week, I felt confident that this place was unlikely to be found unless someone stumbled directly upon it.

The only gap in this shield was the dirt driveway, and that wouldn't do. I found a shovel and dug up saplings of various sizes from the woods, then transferred them in staggered bunches up and down the driveway. I moved loads of pine needles onto the barren dirt to hide the worn pathway leading up to the house. It wasn't perfect, but it would do. The driveway looked like something fading back into the forest through time.

The water well was probably deep and hit some large aquifer, but without a working pump it would be useless. With electrical power now flowing into the house from the repaired turbine, I checked the faucet in the kitchen. I was amazed when it sputtered, coughed and spat air. After a lot more air and noise, it suddenly burst out with splashes of rusty water, then started to flow. After I let it go for a while, it ran clean with cold, wonderful, fresh water. The same luck didn't hold for the hot water, however. The large heater tank had a huge rusty hole at its bottom. As for toilets, I didn't even bother to try them. They were bone dry, and I had no desire to risk filling my new home with my own waste; I could dig my own latrine. Even the stove was electric. Given the situation, the randomness of luck, I couldn't complain. I had electricity, water, privacy. Still, I needed more food.

I found and planted seeds that had been stored in the shed. Squash, corn, tomatoes, onions. But it would be many weeks before anything came of those. The rain helped germinate the seeds, but I needed food now. I found blackberries growing wild, not yet ripe but still edible, near the edge of the woods. During that time, I took up fishing and crabbing — things I'd done from time to time, especially as a kid, but couldn't exactly claim to be expert at. Pillaging the shed outside the house, I found two rods, various fishing tackle, and a faded yellow crab pot. I spent a lot of time, most of my day, fishing or crabbing. Sure, there was the need for food to survive, but also it just allowed me to *do* and not *think*. Even in depression, I realized the bay offered an incredible bounty. With very little for bait, I caught a few small fish. Using those, I caught larger ones, and baited the crab pot. It was a cycle. I could see how the old fishermen and crabbers of decades past could become entranced by its simplicity and ever-revolving truth.

Scouting the nearest other houses, I found a side-by-side double-barrel shotgun, but only seven shells. I went hunting, firing three times at different rabbits before I finally got one. Based on that ratio and thinking how much spray each shot made and still missed, I went back to fishing.

Rather than spruce up the house, I worked at keeping it sound but shabby. The house was small, just one bedroom and bathroom, plus a living room and kitchen, but more than enough for a man planning to be alone for the rest of his life. I kept it nice on the inside, apparently abandoned if anyone caught sight of the outside. Honestly, if anyone had walked up, saw the windmill turning and the crops growing in neat rows and thought the place *wasn't* inhabited, I would've been amazed. But just in case, I kept up disheveled appearances. Checking a mirror in the house one day, I realized I'd done the same with myself. My hair was long, shaggy, and grey, and I now had a scruffy beard to match. I peered into my own haunted eyes, barely recognizing the grey-haired monster in front of me.

It wasn't long before I had company anyway.

2

In the warming spring evenings, I took to rocking on a chair on the porch and watching the sunset, differing blobs of bright orange, red, pink, and yellow dwindling in the western sky. Sometimes the clouds obscured everything and there was just an overall diminishing of light, but even better were the nights that brought a healthy mix of sun and clouds. The warm hues of the sun would bounce off the cool, inverted terraces of the clouds and make for a spectacular light show.

On one such night, leaving late spring behind and moving into summer's real warmth, I rocked on the porch with the shotgun across my lap. A long day of fishing and crabbing in the sun, plus weeding the small crops, had worn me out. Once the sun went down there was pretty much nothing to do anyway. So I drifted off to sleep.

A sudden rustling noise, very close by, startled me awake. Hours must have passed; it was dark. The lights in the house illuminated the nearest surrounding area but cast hideously confusing shadows one layer back into the woods. The branches to my right swayed as if pushed, and I heard the snap of dry twigs being stepped upon. I raised the shotgun. The sounds grew closer, and I strained to see anything in the darkness beyond the lights. In my head, I cursed the fact that I hadn't worked on maintaining night vision, instead opting for the comfort of lights throughout the home. Now my blindness in the dark left me vulnerable.

A step. A second. Pine needles sliding off some unseen form. And then the creature stepped out of the woods only feet from me.

Flicking her ears, the doe looked at me, unsure if I was part of the porch or something alive. She hadn't smelled me yet, didn't know I was there. I slowly aimed the gun at her plump brown frame, thinking of the many days of venison steak dinners that had suddenly been presented to me. Then the deer stepped left and behind her two tiny fawns, maybe a few weeks old at best, appeared from the woods, moving into the clearing. The three walked timidly to the crops I'd planted and lowered their heads to eat the fresh vegetation. I shook my head, unable to force myself to take this mother from her children just to prolong my pointless life. I stood up. Still they didn't notice me.

Walking down from the porch I called out, "Hey! Shoo!" and their attention turned to me. I waved my hands as they approached my small rows of growing food, and the mother snorted. With a deft turn, she bolted, bounding back into the woods, gone in and instant. The fawns rushed to follow, and in seconds there was no trace of any of them, not even a sound. I paused to look in the direction they'd left, smiling despite myself. A tear welled to one eye — sorrow? joy? — and I pinched the arc of my nose to clear my vision. At that moment, I heard a hiss like a gas line broken open just behind me.

I wheeled about and the zombie was on me. Bringing up the shotgun, I had time only to get it between us, then the thing was pushing me backward. I used the barrel of the gun to try to repel the zombie. He — or what used to be a *he* — was huge, with a large round belly slamming into me. He outweighed me by 50 pounds or more. I could smell the filth of his tattered blue shirt and soiled jeans. The rot of his flesh from lesions all over his body. I tripped and he fell upon me, taking the wind out of me with another, louder hiss, his breath blowing into my face like the reek of sewage, his spittle dripping onto me. The zombie snapped at me, we rolled left and right. Angry teeth closed inches from my cheek, my wrist, anything in front of him. We rolled again, but his weight blocked my movement, and he had a clear advantage. As he dug his infected teeth deep into my shoulder, I yelled in pain and pushed harder into the roll.

Now slathering at the open wound on my shoulder, the heavy zombie rolled with me, bits of his leprous flesh falling to the ground. How long had this thing, this *person*, lived this way? We rolled to the edge of the riprap with me on top, and I pushed upward, using the shotgun as a lever. Breaking his hold, I scrambled and stood, hefting the solid gun. The zombie raged at my feet, gnashing his teeth and struggling to lift his heavy form as I slammed the butt of the shotgun into his face. I raised the gun and did it again. There was no need to do it a third time.

I stepped backward, snagging my pant leg on the first of the two steps leading to the small dock, and fell back onto the wood. Sitting there for a moment, I panted to regain my breath. I looked around warily at my torn and bleeding shoulder, the darkness, the woods, the lonely moon above. I thought of the infection seeping into my blood, the death sentence of our world. I thought of my mind slipping, my flesh rotting, my soul leaving me.

After a while, my heartbeat subsiding, I leaned the shotgun on the side of the dock and walked over to the corpse. Stepping behind him, I pulled his arms over his head, trying to avoid breathing the scent or thinking about the horrible texture of the flesh I was holding. I turned the lifeless form around in the grass and managed to pull him up onto the dock. God, he was heavy. After a breather, I continued dragging him until we reached the end of the pier. I considered saying something, some words, some empathy or sorrow for this life I'd ended. Then in a rush, I remembered the zombie that had lunged at me… at us… from another dock, a dream from the past, and I simply kicked the body into the water. It floated for a time, drifting south on the outbound tide. As he gained distance, he took on water and drooped lower into the bay. The wound on my shoulder pulsed, blood streaming out, and I became dizzy, almost falling. I had a vision of this rotund zombie, his face smashed in but still snapping and hungry, pulling himself out of the water and returning to me as I slept on the pier.

I grabbed the shotgun and raced up to the house, locking myself in tight and hoping I wasn't too late.

3

Thanks to Harvey and the people at The Oasis, I wasn't *infected*, I couldn't be infected. But bleeding to death was a different matter. I tore off my shirt. The bite was deep and my provisions were light, or at least lighter than I would have preferred, thinking back to my days as a doctor. I had a needle, thankfully curved, and some regular thread of various weights. In fact, having raided a sewing kit tucked away in a closet of the house, I had many designer colors to choose from. I opted for a good thickness of purple thread — I wanted to be reminded it was there, so I wouldn't forget to check on it and eventually remove it. I had found a bottle of whiskey at a nearby farmhouse on one of my scouting trips. I downed a big swallow of the burning brown liquid, then put my supplies in front of me under the bright lights of the bathroom.

For good measure, I splashed some of the whiskey on the wound, thinking that while I may not be able to become infected with RL2013, I certainly could be infected with something else just as deadly. The lightning shock of the alcohol on my open wound tore through me, threatening to make me lose consciousness. That would surely mean death, and although I no longer cared if I died, for some reason my hands took over, stitching my shoulder back together the way I'd done for countless kids who had fallen off their bikes many years prior. As each stitch went through, the pain of the needle digging through my flesh, the excruciating sensation of my torn flesh being pulled together, I steeled myself and continued. Finally, the gash, while still messy, was closed.

Satisfied with the work, I covered it with a bandage. It seeped blood but didn't gush; I figured it would hold. Staggering into the bedroom, I fell into bed immediately asleep, the full weight of the night's exertion like lead on my muscles and eyelids.

* * *

The next morning, light filtered into the bedroom in waves, and eventually one bright shaft of light landed on my closed left eye. I stirred, groaned, and struggled awake. My shoulder ached horribly, and looking down at the bandage, I saw that the seepage had stained the entire bandage an unpleasant color, like dark, wet autumn leaves, tinged yellow, orange, and deep red. I stood, dizzy and swaying, my mind still fuzzy, and thought of swapping the dressing in the bathroom. Then I heard something outside.

A voice.

"Is it?" a woman asked from some distance.

"I can't tell," a man replied, slightly closer.

Frantic, I leapt up, staggered, grabbed the shotgun, and checked that it was loaded. Had I shot the zombie last night? Yeah, I think I did. Wait, no, it wasn't last night. I was having trouble thinking straight. Shaking my head to clear it, I concentrated. There was a zombie last night, but I didn't fire at it. I broke open the action of the gun and checked. Two shells. Pulling them out, I saw they weren't spent. Okay, I thought, I didn't shoot anything last night. Holding on to that, I reloaded the weapon and closed the action, heading toward the front of the house slowly and quietly. What the hell was wrong with me? This must be fever from an infection, affecting my thinking. Distantly, this mattered to me. Again, I shook my head.

"Looks empty," the man said. I heard footsteps coming closer in the grass. Then a pause. "Hold on," he said. "These are *crops* growing here. This looks new." There was a slight gasp and rustling, I assumed from the woman.

I moved into the living room, peering carefully out the windows. I saw dozens of camo-covered soldiers filing out of the woods. I blinked and shook my head again. They were gone. In their place, I saw only a single man, young, disheveled, a dark mat of messy hair over his rough black beard and flannel shirt. He approached the house cautiously.

Bursting out of the house, I pointed the shotgun at him. He froze. "Hold it there," I commanded. Why was I sweating? Behind him, I saw the young woman, curls of dark hair framing her dirty but clearly pretty face, now showing a look of pure terror. I realized faintly that she was terrified of me. My focus returned to the young man. "You want to turn around and pretend you never saw this place," I said, my voice rough from not having spoken in so long. He stared, eyes wide and hands up, empty palms facing me.

There was a pause. Then… "Please," the woman said. Her eyes shimmered with tears. "Help us."

It was a conspiracy. They wanted to take over the house, they were the government, probably military. I raised the gun. "Get out of here. *Now*," I growled. They both shivered in fear. I could tell they were military spies. I steadied the barrels of the shotgun, aiming at the young man. From my temple, a drop of sweat fell, and I blinked. These were just kids.

"Please," said the man. "We just need a little food, maybe one night. Then we'll leave you alone."

He was trying to trick me. I raged. Stomping down the front steps, I trained the barrel of the gun on the man's forehead. "You need to decide to leave now, or you'll never decide another thing again in your life." More sweat blurred my vision, skewing his terrified face into a mask of deception. Did he think I was stupid enough not to see through his deceit? Blinking again, I saw only two scared young people. I wavered, then held the shotgun high and firm, aimed at his head. Behind him, the woman gasped, and I turned my head toward her just as a young boy, maybe six years old, appeared at her side, clinging to her leg. The boy's eyes bored into me with a haunted look. The joy and innocence of youth was gone; maybe it had never been there. I faltered.

The gun drifted in my hands; the barrel dropped and my mind spun. The man in front of me turned and broke into a run.

"Come on — go!" he shouted, pushing the woman and young boy to flee in front of him, blocking them from me with his body. I looked down at the shotgun as they raced away from me into the woods. I shook my head again. Who was this? This person who threatened children with guns? Was this really me? I blinked again.

"*Stop!*" I yelled. "Stop! Come back!" I meant it plaintively, but it came out gravelly and rough.

I raced after them, staggering. If it weren't for the boy, I never would have caught them. But he was young, with small legs and little stamina. I cornered them in a gap in the pines. "Stop! Hold on a minute!" For a moment we all stood there catching our breath.

The man and the woman looked at me in terror, shielding the boy behind them.

"We don't want any trouble! We'll leave. We just wanted a place for one night," said the man, nearly in tears. I realized my shotgun was trained on them; one simple pull could kill all of them.

Damn it, I needed to get a hold of myself. I lowered the gun.

"Wait, you don't understand," I muttered. The demons in my mind fluttered again so I shook my head, wiping sweat off my forehead. "Take the house," I said.

They looked at me, unbelieving, seeing me waver and shudder in pulses of fever.

"What are you saying?" the young woman said, her tears marring her beautiful young face.

"Take my house. I'm old, I don't matter," I slurred. "There's... there's nothing left for me, anyway." This was the right thing to do.

To give them a chance. I no longer needed a chance, or even cared to have one.

They looked at each other, to the boy, who I assumed was their son, and then back to me. The dawning joy, the elation in their eyes was evident. "Well, hey, mister. We don't need to take it from you. Maybe just share it, okay?" the man offered, stretching out his hand toward me. Why was he *lying to me*? Why was he trying to *steal from me*?

In a haze, I became jealous and enraged. As he stepped toward me, I raised the shotgun again. There was another gasp. The man stepped back toward the woman, shielding her and the boy.

"We need to go," the man said pointedly over his shoulder to his family. The woman nodded, holding the boy tightly. "I think he may be…" The man nodded toward me. I may be… *what?* I thought. Of course. The seeping shoulder wound, the fever, the behavior. He thought I was *infected*. I raised one hand to wipe sweat out of my eyes, clearing my vision. I stopped aiming the gun at them and just held out my hands in a gesture of peace.

"No, no, sorry, really…" Looking to the side, I saw blood dripping down my arm, the bandage badly in need of change. They pulled together and stepped backward, away from me.

I didn't know what to do or say. Suddenly a rush of fever came over me and I fell to one knee, catching myself with the gun as a crutch. They took the opportunity and ran, back into the woods, away from me.

The delirium held me momentarily and I couldn't move. "No!" I shouted. They just ran. I briefly envisioned this family raising their boy safely in my small, secluded house, but they ran away and so did the vision. "Wait!" I said, barely above a whisper. I heard nothing but fading footsteps, rustles on the forest floor.

I reached out, feverishly, toward the sounds growing more faint... and fell face first into a thick pile of pine needles and dirt.

4

Eyes closed, I laid still on the forest floor. Hours passed. The fever did its work. One moment, I felt a chill so deep in my bones that I curled up on the ground for warmth, grabbing my knees in a ball. The next moment, a heat so intense swept over me that I splayed out as if trying to make snow angels in the dirt. Was it four hours? Eight? More? I don't know.

I faded in and out, sometimes eyes open just an inch from the dry brown pine needles, sometimes looking up at the trees as the sun moved across the sky. I dreamt of the young family, huddled in a forest like this one. I watched them as a horde of zombies stumbled across them, tearing apart the parents, leaving the boy alive but infected. My mind fast-forwarded to the boy now a zombie, wandering the woods with mad, dead eyes, looking for me. The chill returned and I balled myself up again on the ground.

Finally, the fever broke and I woke up, filthy from sweating, seeping blood, and rolling in the dirt and pine needles. I looked up at the sky, colors dwindling to darkness as the sun set somewhere off to the west. With my mind finally clearing, I thought about what I should do, what I *should have done*. I vowed to give up the house to the next tired soul to pass my way. Maybe I'd stay a while, help them get settled, but it would be *their* place, not mine. A calm certainty came over me. I knew that once I left the house, I would reach my end. All avenues would have been played out and my story would be over. It was comforting. I'd already come to terms with the possibility of death, didn't fear it. Now I was embracing it, circling it on a calendar almost. Lying there, looking up at the darkened sky, I smiled. I let loose a harsh chuckle, laughing at the pointlessness of everything after all these years.

To my right, there was a sound in response. A low growl.

Turning my head slowing, squinting and blinking to adjust my vision, I saw a dog. When was the last time I saw a *dog*? Low and wide, he stared at me with teeth bare, his coat a mass of curly brown fur matted with dirt, wet in places. He stood his ground, maybe 10 feet away. Keeping my face turned toward him, I used only my eyes to look down at the shotgun. It sat maybe 18 inches from my right hand. I slid my hand toward it slowly. And the growl grew deeper, bubbled into a bark, then back to a growl. The dog's powerful body shuddered, front legs locked in an upside-down V, head low. He took a step toward me and instinctively I flinched. The motion made him stop, unsure, but increased the loudness and force behind his growling. Stretching out, I'd covered half the distance to the shotgun.

Snapping and barking, the dog took three quick steps, almost a leap, toward me. I pulled back, then he did the same. As he retreated, he circled to the left. I lunged for the gun and grabbed at it, then staggered backward and stood, pulling the barrel up in a sloppy aim toward the dog. He barked again as I trained in on his large, shaggy head. My finger settled on the trigger, and in an instant the dog would be dead or dying. Looking into the dog's eyes, I could see the fear, the desperation. A tired soul who had accidentally stumbled upon me and now faced the end of his short, probably miserable life. And I remembered my vow. To give up my house to the next tired soul passing by.

Why was I, once again, ready to inflict harm or even death to maintain my wretched life? A life too long, with no one left in it.

I lowered the gun and flopped down, settling on the ground with a dull thud. I looked at the dirt between my knees, the pine needles tossed in several directions. All of the fight left my body, I became calm. The dog growled, sliding farther left, unsure of what to make of this change.

And then I heard it. Silence.

The dog had stopped growling. Peering up through my shaggy grey hair, I saw him looking at me with his head tilted to one side, curious. Seeing me looking at him, he regained some of his fearful demeanor, a slight growl popping out. I looked down again.

After a moment, I heard him padding across the ground, getting closer, slowly. Without raising my eyes, I lifted one hand slowly. He balked. I froze. Another moment, another step closer. Then I felt his hot breath on my knuckles, sniffing me. He growled again, teeth bare, no more than an inch from my hand.

I just gave up, gave in, didn't move.

And the dog licked my hand.

5

The dog followed me back to the house and I gave him the scraps from my dinner. I grilled one of the rockfish I'd stored in the small fridge, augmenting that with some of the greens and berries I'd collected. Actually, I made too much for myself on purpose, giving the rest to the woeful-looking dog as we ate on the porch. His drooling reached epic proportions, pooling around his front paws as he stared at me. The intensity of his gaze, looking not at me but only at the *food*, was unbelievable. After we finished, I went inside and washed the few dishes, using a little of the water from the tap. I fully expected the dog to be gone by the time I returned to the porch, but there he was. Lying with his front paws dangling off the porch and on to the first step, he surveyed the yard like he belonged there. I took up my customary place in the rocker. When I eventually went to bed, the dog was lying on one side, breathing heavily, asleep.

* * *

In the morning, I got dressed and then stepped out onto an empty porch, feeling an unexpected pang of sadness that the dog was gone. I went back inside and ate a breakfast of dried strips of rabbit — nearly my last — and berries. Sitting at the kitchen table, I couldn't shake the wave of depression coming back over me. I decided to go check the crab pot to have something else to do. I left the house, the front door banging closed behind me, and trotted down the front steps, headed for the pier. About halfway across the distance, I froze. There was a splashing noise. Renewing and increasing my stride, I made it to the pier only to find the dog splashing about in the shallow water past the riprap. He was frolicking and drinking the bay water with glee. I couldn't help the sense of elation I felt. Looking at his curly brown fur, seeming to repel the waters of the bay off its oily surface, I remembered a similar dog owned by a cousin of mine many years before the outbreak. "Chesapeake Bay Retriever. That's what you are." The dog looked up momentarily, then went back to gulping the murky water.

I thought about what he was doing and realized I'd better stop him. "Whoa, whoa. Hold on there, dog." The bay water, though brackish and not as salty as ocean water, would certainly do a number on the dog's digestive tract. "Come here, come on up here!" I yelled, clapping my hands and whistling. He looked up and trotted over, climbing awkwardly across the rocks of the riprap. When he got to me, I looked him in the eye as if to reason with him. "Don't drink from the bay, it's not good for you." As if in response, he shook himself, spraying brown salty water all over the place, and all over me. Wiping flecks of mud from my face and arms, I turned toward the house.

Inside, I walked into the kitchen. Checking through the cabinets and the cupboard, I found an old metal bowl. I filled it with some fresh water and walked out to the porch, placing the bowl down for the dog. He lapped it up happily. "Bet you're hungry, too, eh?" I gave him the last strips of rabbit, but he refused the berries. Worse, he mouthed and slobbered on the fruit, but refused to eat it, leaving me with dripping, gooey berries to consider cleaning or throwing out.

I thought about other food options, knowing this wasn't enough for the dog. He had eaten fish, so that seemed like a good choice. I cooked him up some more, this time a croaker, and he ate it happily. But I thought about how much more food I'd have to catch and store to feed this second mouth. Then I remembered the crab pot.

Checking the pot, I found it full. I dumped all the big ones into a wooden bushel basket and carried them up to the house. I thought I would boil some crabs for dinner, for me and the dog. That day, I tended my rows and did some fishing. Later on, I began work on our crab dinner. After all the prep work and boiling time, and after pulling all the meat out to lay it in front of the dog, he turned up his nose, refusing what I thought was a feast. I ate what I could and stored the rest, making a mental note that fish were okay but crabs were not. This complicated our food situation.

Deer were plentiful in the area, often walking through in the morning and late afternoon. I considered using the shotgun to take one down, providing meat for the dog and me. After a moment's review, I laughed off the idea. First, I wasn't much of a hunter. Second, while my medical training gave me a pretty good idea how to do it, I'd never gutted and cleaned a deer, and the thought of it was daunting, especially at my age. But most importantly, where would I put it all? I had one small refrigerator, with a tiny freezer box on top. I could store 25 pounds, maybe, if I crowded it in with the fish and other stores I already had. I guessed a deer would yield about 50 pounds of meat. Any way you looked at it, I'd be wasting a hell of a lot of meat hunting deer. But rabbit... that might work.

After the dog had been with me for about a week, my supply of fish was dwindling. It was time to try something else. I grabbed the gun and we headed off into the woods toward a clearing where I knew rabbits liked to congregate. I found us a secluded spot on the west side of the open space and we waited. One by one, the little rabbits appeared, heads bobbing in the shaggy grass. I pulled up the shotgun, but none was close enough for me to feel comfortable firing. As I waited for them to get closer, I noticed the dog sit up in excitement. At first unaware of why we were here, now he had seen the rabbits.

Immediately turning predator, the dog slunk down and nosed forward. I dropped the gun barrel, watching him. Inching forward, he got closer and closer to the rabbits as they foraged through the small field, oblivious to what was happening. One rabbit strayed just close enough to the dog and in an instant the chase was on.

The dog turned left as the rabbit arced in fear. Right, then another left. The rabbit alternated swift turns, sometimes flattening its body, sometimes just outright running. The dog leapt after it, tearing up dirt and grass, and the rabbit appeared to be getting away.

I saw that the rabbit would be into the woods in seconds and figured the chase was done. But at the last minute, the foolish rabbit swerved left again and the dog cut off the angle. Suddenly, the frenzied chase was over. The dog closed his jaws on the helpless rabbit and shook his head, over and over, snapping the rabbit's neck. It hung limply out of both sides of the dog's mouth, pathetic and near death, gasping.

Dropping the rabbit to the ground, the dog put one front paw on the pitiful creature, then bit into it and pulled. With a splash of blood, the dog tore the still-living rabbit open and began to pull off bits of warm flesh to eat. I froze.

The sheer brutality of the dog ripping the rabbit apart, the sense of glee with which it happened, was shocking. The clamping teeth biting and tearing living flesh. It reminded me of the zombies themselves. Seeing the rabbit pinned down, being savagely pulled apart, I thought of Rosa lying on the highway, a zombie ripping at her torso, the same brutal intent. Rosa. It was her name that shocked me. Her name welled up in my mind, a name I'd put aside. A name that carried so much pain now. The vision was so clear, it was like I was there, coming around the RV to find them on the street together, and not standing in the clearing of the woods. I squinted and blinked, wishing the vision away.

I couldn't watch. As the sounds of the hideous death continued to play out, I turned and walked back to the house, leaving the dog behind.

* * *

Back at the house, I fell into the rocker on the porch.

Rosa.

I hadn't even thought her name, on purpose, in… how many weeks? Not to shun her memory, but because it was too painful.

Unbidden, I thought of her holding the bullhorn, her last smile. Absently rocking in the chair, I thought of the futility of my entire life. First a doctor, taking advantage of the perks of my position in the community and living off the largesse of the sick and old. Then, when I was needed most, failing to see the full scope of this disease until it was too late. Ten years spent like a rat in a trap. Then Rosa, and hope. But for what? The danger of our journey, yet the hidden joy of *her*, just being there with her. The Oasis. All of our efforts — all of *Rosa's* efforts — to turn a haphazard cure into something viable. And then destruction, everything lost again. She and I in one last mad dash, to a final hope that betrayed us, betrayed *her*.

I saw her head snap back, her blood fly. I watched in slow motion, over and over, the final second of her life. Rosa. Rosa. *Rosa*. I thought of her name, searing it into my mind, accepting it again, along with the pain it brought. I wept. She was gone, and so were my last shreds of hope. Looking down at the multicolored bracelet she'd made for me, I twirled one edge of it aimlessly. Peering closely, I saw a frayed end. Turning the bracelet around, there were more... two, three, four. How long would it last? She was gone. How much longer did this object of her memory have? The idea of it one day snagging on a branch, falling to the ground unseen, left to waste where no one would ever find it again, left me sobbing, remembering her.

The last time I spent with her came back to me, the time when the absolute devastation of her death hardened into thoughtless action. Walking onto the highway, oblivious to gunfire, hearing shouts and commotion from DC. Gathering her in my arms and carrying her to the door of the RV as another bullet tugged at a loose bit of my sleeve. I dragged her limp body inside and placed her gingerly on the bed, watched as her blood drained onto the pillows and sheets. For a moment, I stood over her, watching her in death. I got in the driver's seat and turned the RV around as shots from the DC wall shattered the windshield. Unconcerned with my own possible death, I drove. Heading back south on 395, the RV started to fail. Steam or smoke came out from the engine in short bursts. I knew I wouldn't be able to take it far. I got off the highway, but the next road was too big, too many buildings, too much pavement. I cut across an access road, made turns more by feel than by choice, then turned south again, now on a wooded road just beside the river. The billows of engine smoke became more frequent, then constant. I scanned the area for a place, a good place. Seeing an old, faded sign for a marina, I turned and followed a thin strip of road into a wooded piece of land that jutted into the river. The RV sputtered. I found a secluded bit of field surrounded by woods, and I stopped and turned the RV off for the last time. Billows kept coming from the hood. I stepped back and looked over Rosa's body. But this wasn't Rosa, this humorless, warmthless, lifeless form. I took a last long look, like a scene from a dream, and walked outside, deciding to put her name away in my mind like a time capsule.

Not wanting to simply leave, and having no way to bury her, I chose to make a funeral pyre. I took the small curtains from the RV's windows and tore them into strips, tying some together to make longer pieces. Opening the gas cap, I fed them into the gas tank as far as I could without losing a grip on them. One by one, I placed the soaked rags inside the vehicle. Outside, I found rocks, slamming them into one another until I found ones that seemed to be better at making sparks. I sat inside the RV, reeking of gas fumes, and tried to spark the gas alight over and over, until one finally one caught. I spread the flame around to the several rags, then left, gasping for clean air.

I watched as the RV burned. *As she burned.* She was being burned out of the world, into my soul. "Goodbye, my love," I whispered.

When a dull *whump* announced the first of the explosions, I turned, tears streaming. My feet had started walking, south.

* * *

I noticed that the dog had come back.

He sat next to me, patiently, nosing my arm to get my attention. Had he been there just seconds, or had it been hours? I looked down at him, his muzzle covered in dark blood. Contrasting this reminder of his brutal killing of the rabbit, his face was curved in what seemed to be a smile. His tongue lolled out, panting. Despite myself, I smirked, even chuckled slightly. He was, after all, just a dog.

"Come on," I muttered, gravel-voiced, "we need to clean you up." I led him down to the bay, and encouraged him to wade in. As he dropped into the water beside the dock, a duck leapt out from under the wooden structure, quacked noisily and was scared into flight. The dog was engaged and raced over to the dock. There was another sound under the wood. The dog closed in and I realized a second duck was under the dock, nearest to the shore. It was confined and confused, unable to get out as the dog cornered it. Quickly diving in, his predatory nature returning effortlessly, the dog attacked. I sighed. *Again?* I turned and looked back toward the house, putting my hand before my face.

And behind me, the dog grabbed and shook the duck. I didn't want to see it. There were splashes, footsteps, and an eerie silence.

I lowered my hand, and there the dog sat, directly in front of me. That same odd panting expression, like a smile, was on his face. He looked down, then back up at me. I looked down.

The dead but wholly intact duck lay at my feet. An offering, from the dog.

Again, despite myself, I smiled, thinking of roast duck for dinner.

"The faithful-servant routine, eh, dog?" I asked. He cocked his head to one side. Faithful servant. I reached down and picked up the duck by its limp neck. "You know what? If you're going to hang around, you need a name." I thought it over. "As my faithful servant, I think 'Adam' would be a wonderful name. *Wither wouldst thou have me go, Adam?* You know, *As You Like It?*" I chuckled at the ridiculousness of it. Then, as the midsummer sun waned in the western sky, the dog trotted into the grass, squatted down his hips and urinated. I'd never had a dog before, and had already seen this dog pee many times, but it finally dawned on me. I laughed out loud at how blind I had been.

"Wait a minute, Adam. You're not a boy at all. You're a girl." I paused, considering this. "How about *Addy* instead?"

She barked, as if to confirm the name.

6

Roast duck for dinner. My mouth watered thinking about it. Addy was way ahead of me, drooling throughout the cleaning and prep of the bird. For this special occasion, I decided we would cook outside by the water.

Using smaller rocks from along the riprap, I made a fire circle by the pier, dragging dry wood in from the forest. I'd scrounged some matches from a nearby house, and carefully used them to light some paper under the kindling. The stove in the house was electric and easy, but I clearly needed more practice with starting campfires because it took me five matches to get the thing going. I only had 14 more after that.

The sun was setting across the bay as I gathered my gear for the roast. It was quite the feast. I used some bigger rocks to form an opening where I could rest an iron skillet from the kitchen and tossed in some new potatoes I discovered growing near the garden. For the duck, I made an impromptu spit out of sticks, allowing me to turn it over the fire. I wasn't at all sure how long to cook it, so after a while I started prodding and testing the meat every five or 10 minutes — probably because I was hungry and had nothing else to do. As it got closer to done and the potatoes were softened, I added some peas to the skillet as well. Finally, unable to take the wait any longer, I pulled the duck off the spit and cut it into steaming pieces on a plate right there beside the fire. I tossed a big handful to Addy, and they were gone before they hit the ground, her focus intense on my every move. Grease dripped down my chin as I enjoyed every warm chewy bite of the bird, then sampled the potatoes and peas, savoring the most delightful set of tastes I'd experienced in a long time. The smell alone was divine.

The smell.

I noticed a low pair of eyes watching us from a short distance off in the darkness. Thankfully, I had 50-plus years of exposure to the world prior to the outbreak, so I presumed that the little would-be thief was a fox. I was right. As he circled, taking in the smell, I could occasionally see glimpses of his dirty reddish fur in the firelight. Addy saw him, too, but clearly didn't consider him to be a threat, as she failed to even get up or stop chewing her bits of duck; her only concession to the fox was to turn and follow him with her eyes as he moved. She had no plans to let him steal any of our food.

Suddenly, the fox's eyes darted right and he looked back toward the house. In an instant he was gone, scampering off in the other direction. Moments later, the hackles on Addy's neck went up and she froze. Approaching slowly, eyes reflecting the flames, was a much larger beast, a coyote. A coyote on the Eastern Shore? That wasn't something I was familiar with, but given that the natural world had more than 10 years to rebound from humanity's effects, I supposed anything was possible. It came close enough for us to see its size, around the same as Addy. It sniffed the air and licked its lips. Clearly the roasting duck was broadcasting our presence for untold distances. Addy finished her piece of meat in a gulp and got to her feet, keeping low in that upside-down-V pose, like when I first met her. A low growl began to come out of her throat, and was met by a raspy echo from the coyote. The thing just looked sketchy, like it was built for trouble. It traced a slow arc around the fire while keeping its eyes on Addy, sizing her up. The dog stood her ground, keeping the coyote in front of her as it moved. I looked down and realized the shotgun lay only feet from me. Dropping a bit of duck meat and spilling some potatoes, I set down the plate and reached for the gun.

I knew there were only a few more shells, and the noise of the gun would only add to the attraction of the smell we'd been sending into the forest. I scanned the ground as the coyote took steps closer, gauging. Grabbing a rock about the size of my fist, I threw it, hard, at the mangy beast. It sidestepped and was only barely clipped on one leg. It barked a bit at the affront, still staring at Addy. Finding a second, slightly larger rock, I threw again. This time I scored; with an *oof*, the rock thudded into the ribcage of the coyote. It turned its head my way for once, finally considering me as a threat, too. It let out several deep barks toward me. Addy echoed them, regaining the coyote's attention.

I reached for more rocks, grabbed two, and quickly launched both. One flew just over the coyote's neck, causing it to duck. By chance, the next throw was low, smacking the coyote dead in the forehead with a *crunk*. The coyote leapt backward, uttering a combination yelp and bark. I put out a hand for Addy, trying to keep her from lunging as I grabbed another rock and let fly, hitting a rear paw this time. The coyote, now seeing two adversaries where it had assumed there was only one, turned and retreated into the woods.

* * *

We cautiously resumed our feast, all the while scanning the darkness for sound or movement. Just as we were finishing up we saw them. Walking with a feral mien, two zombies stepped out of the woods and approached. Tall, thin, scraggly ones, both of them. One male in the front, a female farther behind. Their greyish skin mimicked the grey tone of their dirty clothes and hair, giving them a sort of monotone appearance. I immediately grabbed my gun and stood, taking aim but hoping not to use the loud weapon after all this interest in our dinner.

The first zombie, the male, reacted to the firelight, becoming enraged. Loping toward us, he snarled and yapped, himself a human-shaped coyote.

Addy leaped.

In two quick bounds, she covered the distance, flinging herself at him, her teeth biting into his upper leg. The zombie flailed and grabbed at her, diving his teeth into her back as he doubled over on to her. I heard her squeal, saw her release his leg for a moment, then tear into his chest with another fierce bite. The zombie tumbled onto Addy and they flipped, her ending up on top. But the thing had a grip on her now. She made savage rips in his clothing, skin, trying to get free. I couldn't do anything but watch the flailing, spinning fury of it all. Addy bit again, the zombie sunk his teeth into her ear.

Finally, the zombie extended upward and Addy dove down, taking his throat in her jaws. Like a much larger version of the rabbit she'd shaken to death in the field, she held and shook the zombie as he fought to free himself. The vulnerable tissues in his neck ripped apart, blood spraying, and his spine snapped. Like with the rabbit, she shook him again after he was dead, just for good measure.

I sighed with relief, a split second before realizing that I'd lost track of the female zombie. As I turned to scan for her, she fell on me from behind. But that one instant of recognition was enough. I slid down and she overshot me, grasping at thin air.

As she stopped her momentum, I adjusted my grip on the shotgun, grabbing the barrel like a baseball bat. She turned around in a rage and I swung, a *swooshing* sound mocking me as I missed. She dove, pushing me backward, and I staggered, falling down into the nearest of the riprap. A sharp pain struck like lightning in my head, another bolt ripped along my lower back, and I arched with a howl. The zombie kept coming at me, and, in pain, I fell to one side. Pushing up on the gun, I stood and she grabbed me, snapping at me with her jaws, her greasy, stringy hair whipping about. This time, adrenaline took hold of me and I shoved her, feeling a sharp sting of pain in my back. She slid backward in the dirt. I cranked the shotgun in a huge backswing, then let loose, the heavy stock of the gun cracking hard into her forehead, dropping her into a lump. Racing over, I delivered a second blow, straight down, then a third, fourth. She twitched and shook, then came to rest.

I looked for Addy, but didn't see her at first. I needed to get rid of the bodies and smelly duck carcass as soon as possible. I tossed the remains of our dinner as far into the bay as I could. Turning to the corpses, I dragged them along the dock as I had the last zombie, kicking them both into the water and watching them float off.

My heart was racing, but just minutes after the fight and the exertion of cleaning up, I could feel the tightness in my lower back. I touched the back of my head, where the other pain was, and pulled back my hand, wet with blood. Where was the dog? Turning back to find Addy, I saw her lying off to the side in long grass, licking at her wounds. I walked over to her and she stopped licking, looking off into the distance with a glassy-eyed appearance.

"Addy, you with me, girl?"

Eyes flickering in the reflected firelight, she just stared straight ahead, panting hard.

7

I groaned awake. The *light*. Damn, it was bright. Where the hell did all this light come from? I squinted in pain, shielding my eyes with my hands. I rubbed the back of my head, feeling crusted dry blood. My back seized as I sat up, and I winced, dropping one hand to rub the aching spot. With one hand up and one down, I stepped out of bed. I was a mess. I peeked through the hand shielding my eyes to look for the dog, but she wasn't in the bedroom.

I shuffled through the small house, like a zombie myself, looking for Addy. She wasn't in the living room. I went into the kitchen, not seeing her. Then I peered past the kitchen table and found her, lying still on her side on the kitchen floor. As I approached, I could see the matted blood on her fur. A shadow fell beside her.

No, not a shadow.

A smear of blood spread across the kitchen floor. My heart leapt into my throat. "Addy!" I exhaled loudly. She didn't stir. The details of the previous night flooded back to me.

I stepped closer, saw her tongue hanging out of one side of her mouth, motionless. A wave of nausea came over me and I grabbed at the edge of the sink. I vomited loudly for several minutes off and on before the feeling subsided. Surely the commotion woke the dog. Looking over, I saw Addy still motionless. Lifeless.

Noisily, I pulled out a chair from the small kitchen table, a collection of old metal posts with thin padding held together by a flowery plastic cover, and collapsed into it.

Must *everyone die*? Everyone I encounter? Having just started to care again about anything, here was Addy, dead on the floor. I thought of Rosa, lying dead in the RV, of Harvey dead at The Oasis, the other people lost there. Marian, Hank, Janine. Did they all have to die? I put my head in my hands, crumpling out of the cheap chair and onto the floor. I had lived in a shell, as a shell, for so long, then that shell cracked for this dog. This poor sweet dog who died saving me.

"Addy…" I sighed, looking down, feeling the guilt of her death on me.

I crawled over to the dog, slowly, lost in a fog, placing one hand on her body, over her heart.

And she blinked, opened her eyes, and looked at me.

I startled, gasped. Then, in just a second, I laughed. As Addy slowly woke up, I gave her a huge hug, tears dripping into her fur. Tears of joy for a life returned. And tears of sorrow for the lives that could not.

Addy squirmed to get up, and I released the hug. "Come on, girl," I said, rubbing the top of her head. Though she struggled to move, we went outside to relieve ourselves, each in our own place.

Smiling, I couldn't stop the tears from streaming.

8

The next days were rough. The simple acts of moving around, making food, doing the daily chores to ensure food would be there tomorrow… it was everything I could do to get through the day. I must have had a concussion, since my head continued to ache and I found bright lights hard to bear. I made sure to rest more and the symptoms improved over about a week. But my back. That was a different story. I knew that I would heal more slowly at my age, but my lower back felt just about as bad on day seven as it had on day one. Meanwhile, in couple of days you would never had known the dog had been hurt at all. For me, a few weeks slid by in a haze of aches, itchy healing scabs, repetition, but the pain remained.

* * *

One day a steady, soaking rain came. It stayed from late morning well into the night. Eventually tired of being cooped up for most of the day, Addy and I went to sleep early, her on the floor beside my bed. In minutes, we were out.

Clump shhhhh clump…

We both startled awake to near-complete darkness, the rain still pouring down. But that sound wasn't the rain. We knew that sound. Steps on the porch. A zombie? Wandering in the rain?

Addy started to growl, very low, and I grabbed at her, soothing her. "Shhh, girl," I whispered. "Let's just let it move on."

Clump… clump shhhhh clump… clump…

We waited.

Creeeeeaaak… thud.

The door? The zombie had gotten through the front door? Had I forgotten the latch, left it easy to push open? What a mistake, on this of all nights. My heart raced.

I reached for the shotgun beside the bed, still holding Addy quiet. We listened. Through the living room, we heard it move.

Shhhhhhh clump… shhhhhhh clump… shhhhhhh clump…

Addy growled through my hand. "*Shush*, girl," I hissed. We were closed off in the bedroom. Safe, I thought. I tried to hear how many of them there were.

Shhhhhhh clump... shhhhhhh clump...

A sloppy, shuffling sound, now moving into the kitchen. It sounded like just one of them. The sound only came from one place, a uniform pattern. Now, from the kitchen, there were other noises.

Clack clack shikka... thud... shhhhh clack... thud...

What was that thing *doing* out there?

"Stay here, girl," I said, and got up and tiptoed to the door. I cracked the bedroom door and put an eye to the slit opening. I saw nothing but the dark living room; the kitchen was around the corner, out of view. Slowly, I snuck out of the bedroom, slid over to the corner, and tilted my head slightly to look into the kitchen.

There I saw a form. A human form, nondescript, dripping wet from the endless rainfall. Shuffling slightly, it stepped toward the refrigerator.

Shhhhhhh clump...

It wore grey baggy clothes, matching its grey mat of soaked hair. There was a zombie in our home. Luckily, the only light was the muted moonlight coming from the rain-soaked window past the zombie; my shadow, if I even made one, would be cast behind me as I approached. I stepped into the room and slid silently next to the kitchen table. The zombie fumbled for the handle to the refrigerator, tugging, opening the door.

With the butt of the gun held before me like a bayonet, I leapt ahead, aiming the hard wooden end directly at the back of the zombie's head.

It heard me.

The zombie moved quickly, sliding to its left, dodging my attack as the butt of the shotgun slammed into the freezer door. As I fell forward, I looked over just as the zombie reached up, one hand grabbing the barrel of the gun, the other adding to my momentum and pushing me hard into the refrigerator, rattling the old door and the things inside. The force of hitting the fridge stunned me, sending shockwaves of pain through my head and back. I gasped and grimaced, while the zombie took hold of the shotgun and wrenched it from my hands.

It stepped back and turned the gun around, aiming it at my head. I stared, not understanding how this *thing* could do that. Then it reached up and pushed off its thick mane of wet, grey hair in the dim light.

It was a man.

What I thought was hair was actually a wet grey hood, part of the soaked grey sweatshirt the man wore. He was a thin, light-skinned black male, close-cropped hair, very young, maybe mid-twenties, with angry, distant eyes that now were staring at me down the barrel of the gun. My gun. The man was panting, flush from the shock of my appearance, eyes huge.

His sudden surprise and fear turned instantly to anger. After all, without warning I'd tried to kill him. With a rush of fury and adrenalin, he clenched the gun, then steadied it, ready to pull the trigger. Then Addy rushed in.

Swinging the gun as the dog ran forward, I saw in slow motion what was going to happen — he was going to shoot my dog dead in our kitchen. I pounced across the room. Not at him, not to get the gun. But to get her, to get between her and the gun.

Grabbing Addy, sliding with her across the floor until I pinned her against the cabinets, I held her tight. I crouched before the stranger, putting my body between him and the dog. The man stepped forward, shuddering with anger. The barrel of the gun shivered from the way he held it, his grip so tight, white-knuckled, like he was trying to bore his fingers into the thing. But it remained trained on me. Pulling his arms in tight, he steadied the gun and its point-blank aim on my head, breathing hard from the rush of emotions and events.

I looked down at the floor, eyes drooping knowing the certainty of this fate, this death I had somehow avoided so long. Then I simply looked up at him, with a steely stare directly into his eyes.

"If you're going to shoot, shoot me," I said in a voice like liquid gravel.

"But leave my dog alone."

9

I waited for my life to end suddenly, for the light to go out. Or, at least, for the click. The bang.

Nothing happened.

I continued staring into the stranger's eyes, with a cold, hard look. *What the hell are you waiting for, kid?* I thought.

Looking back at me, I saw his resolve disintegrate. He lowered the shotgun.

Voice still full of rough, I said, "Look, kid. You just want some food or a place to stay, I can give that to you." I thought of even giving him the house, but I was conflicted. What would become of Addy? "What's your name, so—?"

"It's... Alain," the kid replied abruptly, looking nervously to one side. "My name is Alain, and don't call me *son*. It just sounds weird. And you're not my dad." He took a deep breath. "Oh, and it isn't 'Alan' — it's *Alain*. Uh-LAIN. Got it?" I nodded.

So now what? I thought. The kid wasn't going to give me his name just so he could shoot me, right? I hoped not. "So... are we all good here?" I asked tentatively.

"What the hell does that mean?" Alain asked, waving the barrel of the shotgun around. "I broke into your house, you tried to kill me, and now I could shoot you dead. 'Are we all good?'" he repeated, mockingly. "Yeah, sure, we're fine."

"Look, son," I started.

"Don't call me son!"

"Fine, fine, sorry. Look. I thought you were, you know, *one of them*, and you can understand why I wouldn't want you in my house, right?"

He considered it. "I guess, yeah."

"So…" I considered the situation. "There's a couch in the living room. Pretty comfortable. You wanna sleep on it, it's yours. Deal?" I held out my hands, palms up, gesturing toward the living room.

He looked at me, so much suspicion. But why? He broke into *my* house. What was his angle?

"How do I know that you won't just have the dog attack if I put down the gun?" he asked.

I wrinkled my forehead with a pondering smirk. "That's a pretty good question, but the dog does what the dog wants." I paused and looked over at her. "Right, Addy?" She looked at me. "Watch this." I gave Addy a stern look. "Sit!" I commanded.

She stood staring at me. Panting with that silly grin.

"SIT!" I tried again.

We waited. Addy ignored the command. "She just showed up here a few weeks ago. I am pretty sure she only answers to herself," I said.

Alain considered that.

"Sit," he said in a firm but low voice. Addy turned toward him and sat, looking up at him with that same goofy grin.

"Of course," I said, rolling my eyes. "Listen, son—" He started to protest, but I put up one hand, stopping him. "I mean, Alain… I'm much older than you and I'm tired. Do you think we can take this up in the morning? The couch is over there. The dog — Addy — and I will be in the bedroom. Okay?"

The stranger Alain waited. Then, as if breaking from a flood of weariness, he nodded. "Okay. But I keep the gun."

10

Another sore, aching morning. My lower back continued to be the worst of my pains, with the added misery of a dull throb in my right cheek where I had hit the refrigerator the night before. I got slowly out of bed and noticed the door to the bedroom was slightly ajar. Addy was nowhere to be found. I went out to the living room.

There, I found them both; the dog, asleep on the floor beside the couch, and above her, this new stranger, Alain. I moved the shotgun into the coat closet, just to keep it out of sight for now, then I coughed lightly and they both stirred. Alain gave a brief start, glancing around quickly before the realization of where he was set back in. The dog just looked at me. I peered out the window to ensure nothing was amiss. The rain had gone, leaving everything soaked. We all went outside to relieve ourselves, each in our own private spot.

Walking back up the porch steps, I called out. "I'm making breakfast if you're hungry." I'd barely entered the kitchen before they both came in.

* * *

"Three mouths to feed," I noted, dividing one of my last cans of beans among three plates. "We'll have to be careful with food, and we'll have to get more."

Alain might have pondered this, or perhaps he thought he wouldn't be around long enough for it to matter. He devoured everything put in front of him. I imagined it had been some time since he'd had a full meal. It was difficult to say who ate faster, Alain or the dog.

As we all sat back, plates clean, I looked at Alain. "Mind if I ask how you got here?"

"I just walked up. It was raining, so I tried the door. You left it unlocked." He eyed me, clearly with disapproval. I sighed. "When I got inside, I thought I'd scrounge for food. Couldn't believe it when I realized your fridge was *on*."

I waved that off. "What I mean is, what's your story? What're you doing out here, in the middle of nowhere, wandering?"

Alain considered the question. He was a cautious person, not timid, but wary. I didn't think he'd say a word, but I guess he must have wanted to tell someone.

"I'm from Norfolk. You heard of it?"

I nodded.

"Well, then you know the whole place is locked *down*. It's not just a walled city, it's a *military* city. There wasn't any way zombies were gonna get in. Too tight." Alain paused, looking at me. "But they did."

"You mean, *en masse*, like an assault?" I asked, incredulous.

"Not exactly. Anyway, listen, I don't know how old you are, mister, but I'm only 20. This zombie shit is all I've really ever known, since I was like 9 years old. In that way, Norfolk was great. You know, we appreciated that it was locked down. Sure, it got old, feeling like you're in a trap all the time, but if you thought of the alternative, well, it was all right. 'Course, now I sit here and wonder if we had it all wrong." He looked around at the house, maybe thinking I had it good here, too.

"Doesn't matter. We had it better than most." He stopped and drank some water, like he was getting ready to share something big. 'The port stayed open. Not as busy as I heard it used to be, *before*, but still ships came and went. Big naval ships on patrol, gas tankers, even cargo ships loaded with metal crates. The Navy would escort the gas and the cargo ships, too, since no one trusted anyone anymore. The world was too messed up."

I leaned in. "The rest of the world…" I pondered. "Still out there." I rubbed the scraggly beard on my chin. Of course they were, but it seemed like a dream, to think there were still people walking the Champs-Elysees, drinking vodka in Red Square, maybe sunning themselves on some Caribbean island. I think Alain saw my wistful stare, my slight smile.

"Don't get your hopes up. The rest of the world is just as messed up as us." I sighed. Of course. "I don't know exactly how many other ports were open, something like two dozen from the lists, I think. I heard stories that before the outbreak cargo ships would bring in things like fancy cars and clothes. What they called *luxury items*. Well, I imagine those ships were still bringing in luxury items, but the concept of luxury got changed. Now, they brought in things like bananas and gasoline. We traded out things we had that no one else had. The biggest was tobacco. People at those other ports would give us a lot of stuff to get some tobacco."

I interrupted. "Where the heck are they growing tobacco?"

"Don't ask me," he shrugged. "Outside the walls, obviously, but you wouldn't catch me there." Then he looked around, at where he was. "Well, you know what I mean." He paused, perhaps not sure where to go next.

"A lot of places really fell apart," Alain said, starting up again. "Japan. Too many people, not enough resources. We haven't heard from them in a *long* time. Anyway, the things that came in on those ships were mostly for the brass — the top dogs in the military. You can rest assured I never had one of those bananas in my life. Not even sure I know what one is. And I'm pretty sure they shipped stuff to other walled cities, DC, maybe Richmond. We certainly brought in more than just our brass could use. Point is, the rich got richer, while all the rest of us lined up for food rations like prisoners."

"So that's what happened," I said. "People got fed up."

"Well, yes and no. We grumbled about it all the time, mocked them and their fancy clothes, fancy food. But like I said, we knew it could be worse outside. That's not the way it started in Norfolk."

"Then what?" I asked, intensely curious now, leaning in. In contrast, Addy ignored us, twitching in her sleep on the floor, probably chasing some rabbit in a dream.

Alain rubbed his nearly bald scalp, scratched at the thin layer of dark hair. I noticed healing cuts in places on his head. "Greed. Too many cargo ships, too many crates. It really had to happen, don't know why they didn't see it coming. They tried real hard to quarantine the sailors when they came in, and they were really thorough, but after a while even a million-to-one shot comes in. Somebody missed something.

"We first heard there was a big brawl in the barracks, some of the younger men, maybe a little drunk on homemade hooch, started something with another group. It got out of hand, all kinds of people fighting. Turns out the ones who started it had just come back from Italy, and they were infected. They got put in the brig to settle themselves down, but by that time you had a bunch of other infected sailors patching themselves up back in the barracks. Within a week, all hell broke loose. Lots of little fighting, meaning lots more infected.

"The military tried really hard to cover up and clean up the mess. There was a big crackdown. They tore through the barracks and gathered up anyone the least bit suspicious. Then they did the same all over the city; seems like they were everywhere, all the time. They found other zombies in the civilian areas, and that just made it worse. So yeah, I guess eventually the contrast between the guys in power and the rest of us is what made the real mess."

"Is the city still standing?" I asked. "Or a total wash out?"

"No idea," Alain said, shrugging. "Someone blew up one of the bridges over the James. The military went even more nuts cracking down on everything. You couldn't move, couldn't even look at them sideways without them getting in your face. And then finally people fought back — there was an uprising. But I wasn't part of it.

"A lot of people pushed to get out. At first I wanted nothing to do with it, but then it became clear that the civilians — all of us — were at risk. People said it was possible the military was going to wipe out all *non-essentials*. We all started to think twice about staying. Finally, when a huge mob pressed toward the tunnel — the Chesapeake Bay Bridge Tunnel — I went with them.

"The first group in was annihilated. Gunned down as soon as they hit the gates. I don't think anybody survived. The second group took huge losses but breached the barricades, made gaps. I was just after that group, which put me in with one of the first groups to make it past the border. We took losses at the gate, too. But most of us survived." He hesitated. "Then we had to get through the tunnel. That was hell. It was dark, pitch black. There were things, living things, down there, I have no idea what. Things moved, some of them running away from us, some toward. Things attacked the group on the sides. We lost a couple of people, some others got torn up a bit. Walking through that darkness was hell on Earth. I have no idea how long it was, but it seemed like about a thousand miles. We held on to each other and pushed through until finally we reached the other side." He paused, looking down, eyes wide remembering. It was clear that what he said didn't do justice to what he went through down in the tunnel.

"How many made it out?" I asked.

"In my group? Oh, I'd say 30 or so. But there were a whole lot more coming up behind us. Once we got back into the light, I decided to leave the group. I thought it would be better to fend for myself." Alain looked up for a moment, studying my expression, before continuing. "I peeled off west toward the bay, scavenged here and there, slept in empty houses. I wanted to keep moving fast, running mostly north, but I had no idea where I was headed, just looking for something with some security." He paused again. "And… and I guess that's it. I ended up here."

I looked the kid over. I was no expert at recognizing lies or half-truths, but I felt Alain was leaving something out, maybe a lot of things. No matter. I wasn't going to push it. While having him around meant another mouth to feed, it also meant having a pair of 20-year-old arms and 20-year-old legs to do some of the hard work around the place. It was settled, at least in my mind. "You know, this place isn't much, but it works for me. If you can stand the couch, you're welcome to it as long as you like," I said. As if in agreement,

Addy finally got up, stretched and walked over to Alain, placing her head on his leg. At first, he looked pleased by the show of warmth, but in a moment his expression changed, becoming harder. He gave me a sideways glance.

"Yeah, thanks." He looked around, almost nervously. "But I think I'll be moving on in a couple of days." Then he got up without another word and walked outside, the front door smacking against its frame as he left.

11

Uneventful days passed but Alain remained. We settled into a routine of household chores, tending the rows, taking turns fishing, baiting and unloading the crab pot. I noticed that Alain was even less familiar with how to do these things than I was. One day, in the mid-afternoon heat, with the sky threatening a thunderstorm, I noticed he seemed particularly flustered. I was weeding the rows and he was supposed to be fishing, but the line had become tangled up with the crab pot and some other debris underwater, making a mess of the thin translucent strands in odd loops and knots.

"How long has it been?" I asked.

He stopped fiddling with the line and looked up at me, still wearing that grey hooded sweatshirt, although it had to have been 90 degrees and humid. "Since what?" he said, sweat dripping.

"Since you left Norfolk."

He stopped. Looked at the sky, thoughtful. "Don't know exactly. But I'd guess two weeks. At least."

"You ever fish back where you come from?" I asked.

He dropped the rod on the dock with a thud. "You wanna do this?" he said, full of annoyance and swagger.

"No, no, no," I waved my arms. "You're doing fine. I just wondered if this stuff" — I gestured toward the house, the crops, the dock — "was familiar to you."

Alain thought about it, looking down at his blistered hands. "Not really," he said after a pause. I just looked at him, face unreadable. "Okay, not at all. I've never done any of this outside-the-wall stuff. How could I?" He threw his hands up in frustration.

"It's all good, son." He started to protest. I held up a hand. "Sorry. Didn't mean to call you 'son' again. But I understand. For most of your life you lived in a controlled city. I'd be more surprised if you actually knew how to fish."

He looked a little relieved.

"What about fight?" I asked.

"Don't worry about that. I can *fight*." His tone was angry, venomous.

"I'm not trying to say you *can't*. I'm just asking if you *have*."

He puffed up. "Oh, I have."

"Zombies?" I asked. He shrunk a bit.

"Well, not really. I've seen 'em. Avoided 'em. But fight them directly, no. No, I haven't. You?"

"Yeah, I have. You see me rubbing my back?"

"All the time," Alain said.

"That's from a zombie — actually two — that walked right into this yard."

"What happened?" he asked. So I told him about the night with the roast-duck dinner. He laughed.

"It isn't exactly funny," I said.

"Come on. You roasted a duck on an open fire and you were *surprised* when company showed up? Maybe just post a sign on the highway, too." He laughed again. I held my face still. After a moment, I cracked a smile.

"Yeah, all right. It was pretty dumb. But, damn, it tasted good." I laughed along with him. "But, back to fighting. I think it would be best if we talked about strategy."

"Okay," he said, "what did you have in mind?"

"They're not immortal, they're not super-human. But if you break one of their arms or legs, they may just keep coming at you, even more pissed off than before. If you're using a bat or something like that, aim for the head or throat. You cave in a skull, the threat is gone. If you have a gun and you're willing to shoot, aim for the middle of the body. Not necessarily because that'll stop them in one shot, but because you don't want to miss. Ammo is in short supply everywhere I've looked."

"Not in Norfolk," Alain joked. I nodded, with a wry smile. "What if you don't have anything?" he asked.

"Run."

"Or if you're trapped?"

"Go for the eyes," I suggested. Alain shot me a look. Did that horrify him? "We should practice a bit. I'll set up something, like a scarecrow. A dummy." He nodded.

We went back to our chores, Alain bent over the tangled fishing line while I plucked more weeds from our garden. A drop fell on my back, then a second. I looked up at the darkening clouds above.

"If you haven't fought zombies, who have you fought?" I asked.

Alain stopped, turned toward me. "Sometimes the zombies aren't the worst enemy out there. Sometimes it's the *people*." In the distance, a peal of thunder cracked across the sky.

12

Summer rolled onward, hot and humid, with regular thunderstorms. During one of the fast, intense storms, a pine fell, striking the side of the house. We found a rusty old axe in the back of the shed and set to work on it when the rains stopped. Alain cut off the branches first, so we could get a clear view of the damage to the house. As he dragged several branches off into the woods, I saw the hole. One branch had connected at a sharp angle with the side of the house, poking a hole into the living room. We could probably live with it, and in fact hadn't even noticed it from inside, but Alain wanted nothing of that.

He was working up a tremendous sweat, chopping and dragging the branches, starting in on the trunk of the tree. "I'd rather not have a hole like that leading into the place where I sleep. Who knows what'll get in there?" He wiped his forehead, covered with perspiration.

"Why don't you take the sweatshirt off? It's hot as hell out here. You'll give yourself a heat stroke."

"I'm fine," he said, clearly flushed from the heat and exertion.

Alain, I was learning, tended to be a tough guy almost all the time. I wasn't really sure why, since I was just an old, scraggly-grey-haired fellow with a bad back. I was no expert at any of this survivalist stuff, just making it up as I went along. And that was obvious. But Alain put on a show like he knew everything, even though you could see him struggle. To his credit, he succeeded. He'd persevere until the job was done, pretending he'd planned it that way all along.

For hours, he meticulously chopped the pine, stacking anything of reasonable size alongside the house. We'd decided that we would need something to help warm the house in the winter. Luckily, there was a small wood stove in the living room. A small stack of logs had stood against the house from before my arrival. With Alain's work, it tripled in size. All the while, he was wiping sweat, cursing, but getting the job done.

Once the pine was completely cleared, we set about filling the hole and boarding it up. We didn't bother making it pretty, just added to the overall shabbiness of the house on the outside. But the hole was closed up, and Alain was happier about that. I supposed I didn't really want a house full of field mice, either.

That night, sitting together at the small kitchen table, dining on fish and vegetables, I looked over at Alain's hands, his long thin fingers, as he reached for a plate. Continuing to chew, and trying not to make a big deal about it, I said, "Hands look pretty roughed up."

Alain reflexively rubbed them together, staring at the blisters that grew large and enraged from his hard work with the axe. "I'm fine," he said.

"Not saying you're not, but those blisters look like they hurt. I know *I'd* be hurting if that was me. Was that your first work with an axe?"

I wondered what he'd reply. Would he keep up the tough act, or actually tell the truth? Thankfully, he went with truth. I guess we'd been spending enough time together that I was growing on him. "Yep. First time."

"What exactly did you do in the city?" I inquired, mouth full of food.

He paused a second, then must have figured that answering wouldn't change anything. "I worked a desk job. OFM. Office of

Food Management. I basically kept track of where the food came from and where it went."

"Explains why you knew about the bananas," I offered.

"Yeah. What about you?"

I stopped, thinking about my past life. From so long ago. Was that even really me? "What did I do in the city?"

"What did you do... *before*?" Alain asked, putting his fork down to look at me as I thought over the answer.

"*Before*," I echoed. "Ah, then." I took another bite. "I was a doctor." Alain's eyes widened, like this was important information he was just finding out. "But don't get too excited. First, I was a small-town doc. General practitioner. Doesn't mean I'm a dummy, mind you, but I wasn't some world-class brain surgeon. Plus, for 10 years I just pushed pills around in a government pharmacy. That's the job they gave me in DC. So, I'm a little rusty."

"Still," he said. "Doctor seems pretty useful, out in the woods like this."

"You know what would be really useful, out in the woods like this? Medicine. I could sure go for some painkillers. I'd love an

Oxycodone tonight, but I'd settle for plain ol' acetaminophen. Without medicines, my options are rather limited. Sure, I can set your arm if you break it, but a lot of choices are out the window now."

Alain listened. Then, as we sat in the glow of the electric lights, he asked more quietly, "Did you have family?"

How long had it been since I thought of my family? "Uh, well... My parents died a long time before the outbreak. Both of my parents were government engineers, a long time ago. They made enough money working up the government pay scale to afford to send me to medical school. Probably wouldn't have happened if I wasn't an only child, though, so there's that. My father died from lung cancer, and my mother went two years later, probably from a broken heart."

"What about someone else? A wife?" Rosa's face appeared before my eyes. Alain must have seen the change in my expression.

"Not a wife. Not ever. I... I don't even know what to call her. But she was definitely someone special."

"What was her name? What happened?" he asked cautiously.

"Rosa. Her name is — was — Rosa." I couldn't help the tears, tried my best to wipe them away nonchalantly, like there was just something in my eye. I doubt Alain was fooled. "We were outside

DC, and they shot her. Just like that." I snapped my fingers, my anger flicking on. I stopped myself, shut my mouth.

"For deserting or something?" Alain asked.

I looked up. There was so much to say, Rosa's life to reveal. "Something like that," I muttered. Wanting to change the subject, I asked, "What about you?"

"I didn't grow up with my parents around. I was nine when Norfolk was closed off. My mother got me and my brother inside before the gates were shut for good, but they wouldn't let my dad in. We were headed to live with my aunt and uncle — my mom's sister and her husband — so we were in good hands. Mom told us she loved us, then she demanded to be let out of the city to be with her husband. I never saw either of my parents again. Growing up with my aunt was fine, she treated us well, but it just wasn't the same. My brother and I missed our parents every day. We knew they died together, outside the walls, separated from their kids." Now it was Alain's turn to wipe his tears. "And my brother was killed on the way out of the city. I guess I forgot to mention that before."

We sat, a couple of grown men, silently crying over what was lost.

"So that's why I just can't *care* about anything anymore. Everything dies. Nothing lasts." Alain spit the words out, like venom, like something he'd been holding in for too long. He was echoing my sentiments, the hollowness of being unable to care.

Then I looked at his hands again. The hands that spent all day being worn to blisters chopping wood to keep us all warm this winter. Alain, me, the dog. I looked around at the walls. The house was feeling oddly like a home.

I couldn't make myself believe Alain didn't care. And then I realized that the same thing had happened to me. I cared again, too.

13

A few days later, we were again sitting at the kitchen table, eating dinner while the electric lights hummed around us and darkness crept over the outdoors, when we heard a strange noise. A splashing sound, mixed with odd grunts.

We flicked off the light instantly, as Addy started a low growl, wary of whatever was out there. I peered out the front window and could just see something down by the pier, splashing in the water. Grabbing the gun, I went to the front door.

"Stay here with the dog," I said.

"I'm coming out, too," Alain said.

I stopped and looked back at him. "Listen, this may be nothing. I go out, see what it is, come back. If possible, I just let it go past, whatever is out there. But if you come with me, we double the chances of being noticed." I looked down at the dog. "Actually, we triple it. She barks, and we're found." I waited for him to agree, not willing to accept another argument. He nodded.

I slipped out of the house as Alain held Addy back and kept her quiet. Tiptoeing into the garden, I used the plants as cover — the corn was growing shoulder height now, so I only had to crouch to stay out of sight.

The sound continued. *Splash splash… errr urk. Splash.*

I finally crept close enough to see, raising the barrel of the gun to put the thing in my sights. It was incredible. A zombie — male, bald, pasty skin, wet and dirty in jean overalls — was splashing through the shallow waters by the dock. What the hell was he *doing*? I watched as he looked around, left, right, furtively, with his milky eyes. Then he thrust his hands into the water with a loud splash.

Was he… *fishing?*

I couldn't believe it. What was this? Was it an indication that, somewhere below the surface, these creatures could still *think*? Or just some sort of natural instinct to eat, to stay alive? I watched the zombie from the end of my gun as he grunted and dove for fish in the dark waters. He staggered closer and closer to the end of the dock. I wondered if he might drown himself simply from lack of understanding, but he stayed back when the water got too deep. There was definitely something going on inside that head.

At the edge of the dock, the zombie staggered in the water. Almost fell. I tightened my grip on the gun. The thing looked into the water, reaching down and pulling at something. Up came our crab pot, full of live crabs. The zombie seemed both jubilant and perplexed. Did it understand what the mesh box was? Did it remember that this was a way to get food? It reached in, but couldn't figure out how to get the crabs out of the wire basket. Blue crabs shuffled side to side, avoiding the zombie's fingers. Finally, it got a grip on a crab and pulled, able to tug it closer but stopped by the mesh of the crab pot. The crab snipped at the zombie, finally pinching a finger in its front pincers. The zombie felt nothing, a symptom of the leprosy, and continued to try to extract the crab.

Another snap from the crab. I saw flesh tear, blood spill. Finally, the zombie felt something, reacted. He smashed at the cage of the crab pot, flinging it back into the water, then raged at the water itself, all around him. He pummeled the dock, tearing apart his hands, before finally calming some. After a while, he moved around the pier, headed south and wandered off. I watched for perhaps half an hour before I could no longer distinguish the zombie from the distant waves.

As I walked back to the house, I thought over what I'd seen. Inside, beneath the raging, irrational surface, were they still *human*?

14

Alain sat with rapt attention, listening to me tell about the zombie in the water.

"Do you think… they could come *back*?" he asked.

I didn't have to think about my answer. "You mean, do I think that a person who has been fully transformed by this disease could return to being a normal human? Be *cured*? No. Not at all."

"Why?" Alain seemed disappointed.

"There are simply too many physiological changes, too much damage done once the body has fully turned, to make a cure reasonable. Even if it were possible to remove the disease, you'd be left with a shell of a person. Their skin would be hardened and damaged, rotted away in places. They'd have limbs torn or broken.

Their vision would be severely affected. Lesions could be treated, but the scars would remain. More importantly, their brain simply undergoes too much internal trauma. Swelling, fever. Even if you remove those symptoms, the *damage* from the symptoms remains. The person would *never* return to what they were before. It's impossible. Speaking as a former doctor, that's my firm opinion."

"But that's just it — it's just your *opinion*," Alain said. "You said yourself that you weren't some big-deal brain surgeon. Maybe someone else knows better than you?"

It was hard not to be offended by the remark, as silly as that was. I was ticked off. "You're right, Alain. I wasn't the most important doctor in the world, no. But you know what I do have that you do not? *Medical training.* That means I know what I'm talking about. Look, I don't want to write off the majority of the human race, either, but facts are facts. Anyone who has fully turned is *gone. Permanently.* There's no hope for them. The only time a person can be cured is before they fully turn."

Alain tilted his head to the side, like a dog hearing a high-pitched sound. "Wait. What?"

I looked at him, confused. "Huh?" I asked.

"You just said, 'The only time a person can be *cured...*' Are you saying there's a cure?" Alain stood up, intensely focusing on me.

I'd said too much. I'd never talked to Alain about The Oasis. About the cure. I kept quiet, looking away.

Alain came right over, in my face. "Hold on, no. You're not going to just clam up now. *What do you mean a person can be cured?*" There was no use in denying it or making up a story.

"Yes, that's correct. A person can be cured." His eyes popped. "But *only before* they're completely turned." Alain backed away. Unbridled joy welled out of him. He spun, looking around, laughing.

"That's *incredible!*" Then he stopped, coming back close to my face. "But *how* do you know that?"

"I've seen it. First-hand." I could see he wanted more detail. "There was this place, called The Oasis—"

"I know about it!" he interrupted. "That's where we were all heading when we left Norfolk!"

"Well, you went the wrong way. And it's gone." He deflated.

"No," he said, shaking his head.

"Yes. It's gone. It was in South Carolina, a place called Hickory Knob State Park. But it was attacked and destroyed. I was there. They had a cure, a real honest-to-goodness cure."

I waited, unsure if I should say it, but nevertheless, I told him. "In fact, I've been cured."

Alain stopped so quickly, the dog startled from her napping on the floor. "No way!" he said, incredulously. "You're lying."

I pulled my shirt down and away, exposing the scars on my shoulder, the definitive shape of a bite wound, healed. "This was a zombie bite, from a few months ago. Before you even got here." He stared at it, unbelieving, mouth agape. He looked into my eyes, back at the wound, then back into my eyes. I pulled my shirt up. "But it really doesn't matter. The cure is gone. Lost. And so is The Oasis."

"This is a miracle," he said, sitting back down in his chair and staring at me. He sat that way for a long time.

15

After that conversation, we kept going about our business, but I could see Alain was always thinking now. Wondering. My news had changed something in him, given him some new form of hope. But I knew that hope was dead and gone. I tried once or twice to reiterate that point, but Alain ignored me.

A couple days later, Alain seemed antsy. "I'm going to head out for a bit, check out other houses nearby, see what I can find."

I just nodded. "Okay." I got the feeling I wouldn't be seeing Alain again, ever. That he was really going off to find The Oasis. The place that was no more. I'd told him just where to look. I figured the temptation was too great.

* * *

About three hours later, he returned. Not a casual reappearance from a routine supply run, but a dead sprint. Alain ran through the woods as fast as he could, racing up to me on the dock. Addy barked and loped beside him as he came up next to me. "What's the big hurry?" I asked, not bothering to even put down the fishing rod.

He stopped, leaned over with his hands on his knees and panted. "There's... a whole bunch... of *people* out there."

I dropped the rod. "Where? How close?"

"To the east, and south. Travelling the highway, but groups were branching off, searching for something."

"Do you think they're heading this way?" My mind raced, wondering what to do.

He considered it. "Yeah. Yeah, I do. I saw them from that red house on the hill south of here. I could watch them as they came up the road. They were using the highway as their main path, but breaking off in both directions. They're looking for something."

I thought about it. "Well, I don't know what they're looking for. But I do know what I don't want them to find." I stepped past Alain and walked quickly toward the house.

* * *

Under an hour. That's how fast we did it. Turned our home into a ghost, a shell.

We'd left the outside of the house shabby on purpose, thankfully, so there wasn't much to do there. The trees I'd planted in the driveway were adding much-needed privacy screens from that direction. But anyone stumbling into the clearing would notice the organization of the place. The neat rows of vegetables in the garden, the tidy dock, the hum of electricity.

We flipped all the breakers, cutting off everything. The house went silent. We dragged rotting branches from the woods and scattered them about in what seemed like a realistic, natural way. We found a little driftwood and littered the dock. But saddest of all was the garden.

In the distance, we started to hear them coming, and Addy perked up, listening.

"Take her in the house, okay?" I said to Alain. "Keep her quiet." He nodded and went.

We had quickly harvested everything we could from the garden. The only thing left was to destroy it.

I walked down the neat rows swinging a rake, lopping off the tops of plants, smashing others. Then I dragged more branches from the woods and dropped them haphazardly over my carefully tended crops. I threw handfuls of pine needles and leaves over the neatly weeded ground. I thought to myself that we might have just sealed our fate anyway; we might have made it impossible to survive the winter. But I continued until the garden looked as shabby as the rest of the yard and house. Then I turned to rush inside.

We could hear people talking, walking, coming closer, not concerned about the sheer amount of *noise* they made. In our clearing, the only sounds were the slow spinning of the wind turbine and the breaking of the waves on the riprap. We huddled in the shadows of the house and waited.

The crowd came closer. Alain and I alternated holding the dog to keep her quiet and looking between the drawn curtains in the kitchen, out the window facing east, toward the sound. Keeping low, we wished for nothing to happen, one big stroke of luck. The talking and the sound of footsteps got closer and closer, no single voice decipherable in the overall din of the group. "How many do you think there are?" I whispered to Alain.

"Gotta be more than a hundred people," he replied. My heart sank. A hundred people, steps from our door. The possibility that they'd just pass us by seemed remote.

I reached out two fingers and slid the curtain to the side, the barest move.

In the woods, I saw a person, red shirt glaring against the natural browns and greens of the trees. He was walking north. Then I noticed another person, a third. They were *here*. I held my breath.

Addy started to growl.

My eyes darted to Alain, and he leapt toward the dog, landing as silently as possible. We'd both gotten caught up in looking out the window and left Addy by herself. As Alain grabbed her to quiet her down, she let out a small bark.

We froze.

Alain held the dog's muzzle and she looked wide-eyed up at him. After a moment, I turned and looked outside, terrified of what I'd find.

More and more people streamed by, some distance off, weaving through the pine trees.

But no one came closer.

We waited. In time, maybe 20 minutes, we could tell the mass of the crowd had moved north. Stragglers continued through for a while. We didn't move, almost didn't breathe at all.

Finally, we realized we hadn't heard any noise in some time. But we waited some more. Over an hour later, Alain spoke. "I think they're gone."

I didn't want to move, or acknowledge it, for fear of being wrong. I looked out the small slice between the curtains again. But I had to admit, there hadn't been anything for a long time. "Yeah, seems that way. Where the hell did that many people come from?"

Alain looked at me. "Norfolk. That'd be my guess."

He let go of Addy and she jumped up, shaking her whole body like she was ridding herself — ridding *us* — of the weight holding us all down.

* * *

Another hour passed and there was nothing. We breathed a sigh of relief, even laughed at the whole thing. "I'm going to make dinner," I said.

A short while later, I plated up croaker and corn for myself and Alain, after deboning another croaker and tossing it to the dog.

"You wanna sit outside?" Alain asked.

"Sure," I said, holding out his plate for him. He took it and walked toward the living room.

As I turned to grab my plate and follow him, I heard a crash. Addy and I ran to the front door, where we saw Alain standing, blocking the open doorway, hands empty. Below him, shattered on the threshold, lay the broken plate, food spilled all over. Alain stared out the door.

I approached and tilted my head to see past him.

There in the yard, just steps from the porch, stood a man.

He was large, imposing, in jeans and a flannel shirt, with rough, dark beard and shaggy hair. Most notably, he had only one eye. The other was an empty socket. Then I noticed a second man behind him, blond, skinny, tattered t-shirt, dirty jeans. They both looked at us. The bearded one — the one-eyed one — smiled, showing a mouth of yellowed, rotten teeth.

"Well, hello again, Celia," he said.

16

"Celia?" I echoed.

Alain, as if waking from a dream, turned past me and went back into the house. I just stood there looking at these strangers, here in *our home.*

"Who's Celia?" I said, distractedly, slowly turning.

Addy took notice of the men, felt something amiss. She growled. The one-eyed man hefted a large, heavy stick, holding it like a bat. "You're gonna wanna hold yer dog," he said, nodding toward Addy. I reached toward her, but she jumped, flying down the porch steps. She leapt to attack the one-eyed man.

He swung.

Addy let out a high-pitched yelp and crumpled to the ground, broken. The second man rushed up, also brandishing a heavy stick.

"Stop!" I yelled, rushing down the steps toward Addy's motionless body. Behind me I heard footsteps on the porch.

I turned and saw Alain, lifting the shotgun.

"Hold up! Wait!" shouted the one-eyed man. His partner pulled up quickly, maybe 20 feet back.

Like a clap of thunder in my ears, Alain fired the gun. The one-eyed man was propelled backward, riddled with pellets. I heard him exhale a giant *oof!* as blood splattered the clearing. He fell, forever silenced.

The other man paused for a second, looking down at his fallen friend. Alain swung the gun past me, past the dog, to face this second stranger. The man looked up, eyes bugging, and Alain fired again.

The shot was wide, grazing the man with a few pellets. He turned and ran back into the woods, bounding left and right through the trees.

Alain broke the action of the gun, popped out the used shells and reached in his pocket for new ones. He fumbled, too unfamiliar with the process. It was too late. The man was gone. I rushed to Addy.

The dog winced at my touch, but she was alive. Alain walked over with the shotgun, barrel dangling down.

I felt Addy's body. Broken ribs. I hoped none had punctured a lung, but there was nothing I could do. I looked at Alain.

"Celia? Who's that?" I asked, reeling from the rapid-fire events.

"Me," he said. I looked at him sideways.

"You're a woman?" I asked.

"Is that a problem?" he — no, *she* said.

Raising my hands, I replied, "No, no. I just… *had no idea.*"

"That was kind of the point, genius. But now, we have to leave."

The realization hit me like a punch to the gut. There was a man running free, probably an offshoot of the large group that had passed us. He knew we were here. He'd want to avenge his friend. And they'd all figure we must have some supplies they'd want, too.

"The guy you shot. How did he know you?"

Alain — I mean, Celia — looked into the woods with a face made of stone. "There's no time now. There will be others. We need to leave." She looked down at the dog. "Is Addy going to make it?"

I nodded. "I think so. Unless she's popped a lung, but for now, I think she just has a couple of broken ribs."

"Then come on." Suddenly Celia was all business. "We gotta pack up."

We grabbed bags and filled them with extra clothes, food, lots of water, other supplies. We were weighed down, carrying everything we could. Addy stood up, wobbly, but she could move about. We gave her some water, and she drank it.

Celia. How did I never see it? She'd covered herself in that grey sweatshirt, her hair gone, her face grimy and harsh. What before seemed to me to be a thin young man was suddenly revealed to be a young woman. I stopped for a moment, thinking of all the things we'd been through, the chores, the hard work, the downtime, the conversation. And yet, this.

"Is the rest true?" I asked.

"The rest of what?" Celia responded.

"Your story. Norfolk. Your brother. The uprising. The group that left in the tunnel."

"Yeah. It's all true. Alain was my brother's name."

"But why the secrecy? You've been here for weeks."

She looked at me, cold. "We need to go. Now." She picked up her bags and pushed past me out the door.

We left the house, a sanctuary for so long, and never saw it again.

17

Woods. Hills. Fields. They all went by in a blur. My back ached, I was carrying so much. But we plodded on. Addy limped beside us, willing to endure whatever she must.

Celia led the way. I followed, blindly, trusting her to choose a path. My mind wandered.

How? How could this happen again? Just when things had become *good*.

This world we lived in was too much to bear. I found myself falling into a depression, unable to even contemplate the thought of starting over, yet again, somewhere else. For what? How long would that peace last?

Celia. What did I really *know* about this person, anyway? If she'd kept such simple things as her gender, her name, from me, could I really trust her? She felt like a stranger to me, albeit one who looked just like someone I knew.

And the dog. Poor Addy, struggling to keep up with us. Maybe she should stop, maybe we should leave her to fend for herself. She'd done it before. Or would that be a death sentence, leaving her behind, injured? There were times when she drifted back, even out of view, and I thought that would be it for her. But she always managed to catch up.

I could feel the weather changing, the approach of fall. The approach of our downfall. Living through one winter outside the city had almost killed me. I felt certain a second winter would finish the job. So why try? Where were we going, why did anything matter?

It was a long day on the road, heading nowhere, from what I could tell, but as it came near dark, Celia approached a house. She carried the gun, waving at us to wait as she went to investigate by herself. Addy and I were more than happy to stop.

Celia silently padded up to the house, then circled it. She went to the front door and tried the handle, but it was locked. We saw her circle around to the back again. Then, nothing. For several long minutes.

Finally, Celia opened the front door, gesturing to us. "Come on," she said.

It was a hovel compared to the house we'd left behind. This one was bigger, two stories, but empty except for debris. No furniture. We checked, but there was nothing in the way of food or water. It would just be a roof. We ate a bit from our packs, in silence, then each found an open spot of floor and went to sleep.

In the morning, I went to Addy, wanting to see how her ribs were doing. She eyed me carefully. I reached out and touched her side, where the stick had caught her. Addy flipped quickly onto her feet and snapped at me, canines chomping inches from my hand. I moved backward quickly. There was a strange look in her eyes, one I didn't like. But she'd been hurt. I remembered that animals would often lash out when injured. I let it go.

The next day was much the same, with another empty house that night. They blurred together, meaninglessly passing us by, meaninglessly marking our progress toward an unknown destination, for an unknown reason.

18

Another night, another abandoned house, less food, less time.

We spoke during dinner, really, for the first time since we had started this journey to nowhere.

"Those men. The one you shot, and the other," I said wearily. "How did you know them?"

Celia the woman put up the same hard exterior as Alain the man. She looked at me, as if she were gauging whether to speak. But I could see she was tired, too.

"They were part of the group I came out of Norfolk with. They were in the tunnel." She went back to eating.

"Well, then, I guess I can see why you left that group."

"The big one. The one with only one eye?" she asked, keeping her head down, eating.

"Yeah?"

"He raped me. The other one helped. Just over a week after we got out of the tunnel." I opened my mouth to reply and stopped. Now it made sense. The shaved head, heavy sweatshirt, pretending to be a man. Celia had been through something no one should ever endure, and clearly she had no intention of letting it happen again. No doubt she looked at me with suspicion as well. What man could she trust after that?

"I'm... sorry," I said, trying, failing, to say something of use. "I thought you shot him because of what he did to Addy. But now I see..."

"I *did* shoot him because of what he did to Addy. And also for what he did to me." We sat in silence for a while.

"I know you're not asking me for more of the story, but I don't want to keep it to myself anymore."

I just nodded, letting her find her own path there.

"The big guy with the beard was a loudmouth. A trouble maker. Named Burt. The other one was your typical sidekick. Weak. Mean. I don't even know what his name was. He only had any power at all because he would do whatever Burt wanted. They knew that together they were more intimidating.

"We had a group of around 30, like I told you. But most of those people were scared, tired. In Norfolk, they had worked desk jobs, like me. None of us ever planned to be outside the walls, no one was ready to take charge. That meant survival of the dumbest, or at least the biggest oaf. Burt was a pretty big oaf. He shot his mouth off about where we should go, everything we should do. When people would dissent, he'd have the other guy back him up, act like it was a group decision."

Celia's voice picked up a little, became stronger, like she was leaning into the story. "It didn't take long before he was becoming a true tyrant, having his way in every way. And then he wanted something else. Me. He approached me several times, first trying his ugly attempts at charm, his witless version of coming on to me. It was hideous. I considered the possibility he might attack me, but dismissed it. We hadn't fallen *that far, that fast* already, right?"

She stopped, looked at me. I didn't say anything. She nodded, then started to talk in a lower, emotion-filled voice. "We had. One night, as I was about to go to sleep, Burt approached me from behind and grabbed me, and he and the skinny little bastard dragged me into the woods. Burt raped me. I only wish that I'd fought back sooner. But I did fight back, eventually. When I finally snapped, I screamed and shoved my thumb into his eye. Burt's eye. You saw the results of that. He yelled and yelled, acted like he was dying. Screamed curses and threats at me. I just wish the sonofabitch *had* died then."

I shook my head, unable to truly fathom her pain.

"I took off, running. And I just kept running. As long as I could, for days. I tried to sleep here and there in houses, but I kept hearing Burt coming up behind me again. Thought I could even smell his foul breath on me. His rough hands. When I did sleep at all, I dreamed of him. In some of my dreams, I killed him. In others, he kept raping me, endlessly, until I think I died. When I finally got to your place and you snuck up behind me, well…" She turned her palms facing upward, like, *what did you expect?* I just looked at her, having no words.

She looked dead straight at me with a cold expression. "But now Burt is dead, and I'm determined to make sure that *no man — nobody* — will ever take advantage of me again."

19

When Celia thought we'd gone far enough east, she turned us north. I followed without question, allowing myself to be freely directed for the first time in a long while. I vaguely considered that north was the direction the mob had gone, but figured we'd traveled far enough inland to avoid them.

As we plodded northward, Addy wandered off, agitated, acting strange. I wondered if she'd come back. This life of constant walking must have seemed so unusual to her. I considered how little *I* knew about where we were headed, then compared that to Addy. She truly had no idea what was going on.

Addy was gone for more than a day. It seemed like she would follow us on the fringes, able to return when she wanted, but otherwise she remained out of sight. Celia and I assumed she was hunting, finding something with more sustenance than we could provide. Our bags dwindled, even though we ate and drank as little as we could. Eventually we only needed one bag.

When Addy finally returned, her eyes seemed lighter, stranger.

One day, we approached Route 50 from the east, and carefully scanned the highway from the shadows of the trees. I vaguely remembered taking this road before. We saw nothing in any direction, so we followed along the road to speed our progress north, staying to the edge.

Celia eyed the many abandoned cars and trucks longingly. "We should get a car," she said.

"I did that once, on the way to The Oasis. I seriously doubt that lightning will strike twice." As usual, Celia didn't take my word for it, stopping to check car after car. In cases where she could find the keys, every battery was dead. I told her about the RV and having to charge the battery overnight with a generator. I thought that would dissuade her, but instead she started to look for battery chargers, generators. It was fruitless.

My back was a terrible hindrance, forcing us to move more slowly than Celia wanted. With the dog often wandering off alone, and me limiting her progress, it was a wonder Celia stuck with us. I have to wonder how things would have turned out if she'd simply decided to *go*.

As one day turned into evening, the chill of fall in the air, we came upon a farm along the side of the road. A large barn stood off to one side. Celia investigated the house first, but came back with bad news. "Full of mice, maybe thousands of them; smells like mouse turds," she reported. We checked out the barn instead, just as Addy came into view.

The barn was empty, except for some old straw on the floor and more in the loft above us, perhaps 12 feet off the ground. We spotted a ladder. After talking it over, we thought we'd have a more peaceful rest up above. "What about the dog?" I asked.

Celia shrugged, not an offhand, *who cares?* kind of shrug, but the deflated kind. No good answer came to her mind or mine. *What else can we do?* In the end, we ate our light supper on the floor of the barn, then as the moon rose, we closed the barn doors and were left in darkness. Celia and I went up to the loft, me struggling to pull myself along the ladder as my lower back spasmed. Addy stayed below. I felt awkward about it, like I might be betraying my good friend, my faithful servant, this dog who had been nothing but good to me for so long.

In the middle of the night, there were strange noises. Celia peered down into the barn's main interior, but said she didn't see the source of the sound. But she did see Addy sleeping motionless throughout the noise, on the rotting straw floor, as a single line of moonlight fell across her from the crack between the barn doors.

20

I awoke in a world of pain. My lower back had seized during another night of harsh sleeping, causing me to pull myself into a ball, trying to stretch in some way to provide relief. It was useless. I was useless. I told Celia to leave without me, that I wouldn't be able to move at all that day. She looked at me, looked aside. I could tell she was considering it, hard. In the end, though, she stayed.

Addy slept very late, hardly moving. Finally, in the late morning, she stirred and we gave her some food and water. She seemed jittery. It was unlike her. I was deeply concerned, having an idea of the problem but not wanting to voice it. Was this rabies? Or, was it… something more? The very thought made me shiver.

I remained in the loft all day. Celia went out, perhaps to scout ahead or check nearby for supplies. She came back late. I don't know if Addy was around or not, considering that I spent most of the day huddled in a ball or asleep. My age felt like it had crept upon me, latched on, and wouldn't let go. I had troubled dreams of Addy, wondering what she was going through, imaging horrors too great to describe.

* * *

We had a small meal late in the afternoon. The day of rest had helped me out, but now I was trying to work out the kinks of sitting idle for too long. I had insisted on climbing down the ladder and eating with Addy. As I heaved myself down beside the dog, my back let out several loud cracks in succession. Celia looked at me with a raised eyebrow, and I shrugged. Addy sat with us as we ate, absently taking small morsels from my hand.

After the meal, I felt surprisingly tired. I tried to play it off for a while, but there was no use. Addy was already asleep again in a corner of the barn. Celia closed the barn doors as I went to the ladder and climbed back up.

In the night, we again heard a strange series of sounds. Hisses, yaps, snarls and growls. Celia once more scanned the barn for the source. I joined her, having improved the condition of my back with a day of rest. We sat, side by side, looking for something, anything, in the darkened hulk of the barn.

To our left, the sound continued. To our right, something took form and moved below, walking out into the center of the floor. It was Addy.

The sound grew and came in closer, from the left. Addy looked in that direction, almost in a fog. Then, two large, puffy raccoons skittered in. The smaller one had half an ear, the rest clearly missing from a bite. The two creatures seemed very confident, familiar with their territory. We could almost see their distaste for Addy, as well as their lack of fear. They approached her, clearly in the process of preparing an attack. They stepped forward, slid sideways, circled. Several times they bumped into each other and started up that *sound* again, raging at each other. A front paw, claws out, slashing. The same, mirrored. The raccoons were angry, feral, ready to fight anything, and they approached Addy without fear. Addy looked weary, perhaps unconcerned, perhaps unaware.

As we looked down from above, the raccoons circled Addy in the middle of the barn floor.

Addy, easily heavier than the two raccoons put together, tracked their circles but couldn't escape the movement of both of them at the same time. As one circled away from her, the other moved in. A slash. Addy bled. She let out a yelp of pain, coming to her senses enough to begin defending herself.

We just *watched*.

Addy stood her ground. The two raccoons took up places opposite each other, with Addy in the middle. She would face one, be attacked by the other. The three circled together, like fates intertwined.

The half-eared one lunged from behind, striking Addy in the meat of her back leg. Her flesh was torn open, bleeding.

I'd had enough.

I looked at Celia. "She's *ours*," I said. She nodded.

Without another word, we rushed to the ladder and slid down. As my feet hit the ground, a jolt of pain flashed up my back. I ignored it and grabbed a pitchfork that had been discarded nearby. Celia raised the shotgun. The light was dim, so I stepped over and threw open the barn doors, letting a wide bath of moonlight flood the interior.

The light fell across Addy, and she *changed*.

She turned toward us, as if the light was burning her, causing her pain. It was only the pale glow of the moon, but compared to the darkness inside the barn, it seemed bright. Addy suddenly raged, turning her head left and right, shaking her body.

The smaller raccoon with the half ear chose to lunge at her at just that moment, nipping at her hind leg. Addy wheeled, leapt on the raccoon, and savagely bit into its neck, behind its ears. The thing uttered a horrific, snarling wail as Addy tore the life from it. Like she'd done while hunting that poor rabbit, she clasped the raccoon's neck in her powerful jaws and shook, snapping its spine. The raccoon fell dead at her feet. Then Addy turned toward the other, still shaking her head with rage, like she was trying to get the madness out of her by sheer force.

The second raccoon, perhaps the smarter of the two, turned to flee. It raced across the floor of the barn, but Addy wouldn't let it go. She pounced and bit, severing its tail from its body. The raccoon yelped but still tried to escape. Addy grabbed it by a hind leg. The raccoon railed against her, full of terror and fury. Addy dropped it, and it spun on her in self-defense, snarling with teeth bare, spittle flying. Addy ignored the show of strength, as well as her own safety. She stepped forward and, as the raccoon bit her repeatedly on the face and neck, she dove for its underside. The smaller animal flipped over unwillingly.

The dog, now seemingly alien to us, a wild beast, went for the kill. She chewed at the raccoon repeatedly, without mercy. As she turned away, it lay gutted and writhing on the dirty floor, its blood seeping into the matted straw.

Then Addy looked at us.

The cold steel of fear penetrated my body like a weapon, as I saw Addy's eyes. Not the warm brown eyes of the dog to whom I'd thrown food scraps for many months, but greyish eyes glowing in the moonlight.

She walked slowly toward us. We could see countless bite marks, bleeding dark blood into her disheveled fur. She shook her head again, but just slightly.

Addy walked past us both as we stood dumbfounded by the barn door, and padded back to her bed, leaving bloody wet paw prints all along the way.

21

We climbed back up the ladder wordlessly. In the loft, I turned to Celia with a pained expression.

She thought for a moment, then slowly whispered, "Do you think...?"

"What? That Addy is sick? That maybe it's rabies?"

"No. Well, not exactly. Do you think she has... *the disease?*" Celia asked, wrinkling her brow as she leaned in to emphasize the question.

"Rabies is capable of being spread between different mammals, like a person infected from being bitten by a rabid animal," I said. "But I don't think leprosy spreads between different species, even though there are leproid diseases for cats and dogs." I sat and mulled it over. "It would be fairly rare for something like RL2013 to jump species. But... I suppose it's possible." The idea left me reeling.

"If she is… how?" Celia asked, shocked.

I thought about it. The raccoons Addy fought couldn't have infected her so quickly, and they actually didn't seem infected themselves. So then what?

I thought of the night we had roast duck.

"You've seen my shoulder, where I was bitten. That night, there were two zombies. Addy killed the other one, but not before she'd been bitten several times." It was the only thing that made sense. How long had it been festering, latent? Was that possible?

And if this was true, what did it mean for the rest of the world? If the disease could spread to other species, what effects would that have? I imagined a chain of preposterous entirely imaginable events, like an infected wild dog attacking livestock used to feed the cities, spreading the disease back into the last bastions of safety left in the world. If that were to happen, only the loners would be left, pinpricks on the Earth's surface, barely noticeable. And as I well knew, survival in the wild was hard. I hadn't even made it through two winters yet. If the disease spread as I began to fear, it could well mean the final death knell for the human race, and many other species, too. Like Earth was being rebooted.

I stared down at my hands. My empty, useless hands, unable to do anything for even the dog below me, much less for the entire world.

Celia considered things for a moment. "If dogs can catch the disease, too, where does it end?" She looked at me, knowing I had no answer, but pleading with her eyes anyway.

"I don't know. Maybe it doesn't end," I sighed. "Maybe we do."

Below us, something stirred.

Addy.

She scratched at the floor in her sleep as we peered down at her. Slowly at first, then with growing strength, we heard a woeful sound. A long, low, rising howl came out of her, even as she slept. As the pitch rose, her eyes opened and she stirred awake, seemingly unable to stop herself from making the sound. She stood on jittery legs, head down, as the pathetic noise grew louder.

I looked at this poor dog. A dog I had become responsible for. My friend.

"I have to do something," I said in a low voice.

Celia turned to me. Even in the thin light of the barn, I could see her eyes fill with tears. The barn doors remained open, forgotten after the events of the evening. The entire place had a haunted, dim blue glow. "What can you do?" she said with a hollow voice.

"I don't know. Anything. Sit with her. Comfort her."

"She's not Addy anymore," Celia said. "She might..." I knew what she might do.

Below us, her pained wail increased.

I crumpled, shoulders falling. I knew it was true, that I could do nothing. But she was my friend. Why was this happening? Why this dog, this poor damn dog that just wanted to splash in the water? I squeezed my eyes closed and imagined us back at the house, playing in the shallows of the bay, Addy endlessly retrieving sticks as I threw them from the dock.

"Then I'll have to kill her. To put her down," I said, hating the words coming out of my mouth. Celia gasped, but didn't reject the idea. We spent a moment staring at each other. Did either of us have the strength to kill our companion, even if it was out of mercy? We wavered.

And then, finally, I decided it had to be done. If Addy was truly gone, then the monster trying to replace her had no right to live in her body, to take her form. I turned and picked up the gun.

As I stepped toward the ladder, Addy's horrible wailing stopped. Celia and I looked quickly downward, just as Addy began to shake and twist.

She turned in half-circles, she bumped the walls. I lifted the gun and put my foot on the ladder, determined to end this misery.

Whether Addy sensed some danger or just fell into a madness, I couldn't tell. Turning toward the open doors, she fled.

A short while later, we heard her moaning howl again, from the east, fading.

22

I held my hand out toward the barn door, as if that alone would return Addy not just to the barn, but to her old self. But she was gone.

I dropped the gun onto a rotted bale of straw in the loft and collapsed.

Celia came to my side, putting a hand on my shoulder. "Addy was a really, really great dog. But that isn't Addy anymore."

"We don't know anything for sure," I said, angry and irrational. Knowing that we really *did* know all we needed to know.

Celia grabbed both of my shoulders with her hands and turned me to face her. She was crying, tears streaming freely down her face. "Listen. I love Addy. When I ran into you two, after that first night, she took to me right away. You know what I went through with those bastards, that man Burt and his friend. I trusted the dog more than I trusted you. You were just another man. Another somebody to keep my eye on. But the dog, I could just love."

"You're afraid I might do something to you?" I asked, stunned.

She shook her head. "No, not now. Not for a long time. You're a good man. You really care about people."

"Me?" I scoffed. "Care?" I couldn't stifle a sarcastic laugh. "I holed myself up, alone, in the woods, scared, hiding. What people did I care about?" I shook my head.

"Her. I know you cared about her. *Rosa*," Celia said. It was the first time I heard Celia ever say the name. "And then she died and you needed to be alone, so you were. For a time." She looked right at me, her brown eyes glinting in the filtered moonlight. Near bald and mostly dirty, Celia held herself like a queen. Proud. Then I realized she *was* proud, of *me*. "But then a dog came along, and that dog would've died on its own. You saved her. Addy. And later a person came along, and you could've just shot me. I don't mean just the first night, but any time. Or smothered me in my sleep, or whatever. But you didn't. Instead, you gave me food, water, a place to stay dry, warm. Not since my aunt and uncle back in Norfolk has anyone *taken care* of me." Her lips quivered. The tears kept flowing. I wiped my eyes, noticing that I'd joined her. I looked down, embarrassed and ashamed to hear so much praise.

"Why is life *like this*?" I asked. "Why?" I balled my fists into my eyes, then turned and looked at the rafters of the barn. "We fight and fight, and sometimes we meet someone we care about... and then..."

"And that's the *reason* we fight. We fight because we *have to* have those moments. Those people we care about. Otherwise, it's all shit." Celia waved her hand at the barn, the world.

"Why Addy? Why that poor dog?" I asked no one. Then the idea came to me, strong. "I have to go find her. To do the right thing. The thing I was about to do here."

Celia shook her head. "How? You'll never find her out there, not unless she wants to be found."

"Well, I have to try."

* * *

The next morning, I gathered my gear. The gun. Some of our supplies in a knapsack. Celia did the same.

"Which way are you headed?" I asked her, just making conversation as I put things in order.

She pulled up. "With you," she said, matter of factly. I turned and looked at her, frowned.

"No. Come on. This is my responsibility."

"Stop," she said. "I love Addy, too. I'm coming with you."

"But—"

"But what?" she asked. "It isn't like I knew where I was going anyway."

I couldn't help but laugh.

* * *

We were ready to go before the morning got late, stepping out into the yard beside the barn. We took only one bag, our supplies were so light. We pointed east, away from the barn, the farm, the highway behind it. Ahead were woods and unknown.

As we crossed the small clearing and stepped into a thicket of trees, we heard an unusual and unwanted sound: *people.*

I knew instantly it was the big group that had passed us at the house. Moving faster because it was just the two of us, we circled them, east, then north, coming up the highway ahead of them. Now, after our days in the barn, they'd caught up. More and more we heard them. People ranging to our south, east, west.

We ran north, away from the sound, and into the dry fields of corn.

23

Yellow. Everything around me. The drying stalks of corn, withering unpicked. The clouds, looming in the late morning. In the distance, the yellow leaves on the trees signifying that fall was here in earnest.

The wind blew across the fields as we made our way north to avoid the refugees from Norfolk, tramping along somewhere behind us.

Ripples chased across the dry stalks, making waves of movement and a hollow rattling sound like the clacking of skeleton bones.

Celia ranged out in front of me, her grey hood up over her head and carrying the gun while I toted the last of our supplies on my back. As she crested a hill in the cornfield, she turned to look back at me. I gave her a half smile, to tell her that my sorry old bones were keeping up with her, able to carry the load. She smiled back, then turned away. In that moment, she reminded me of Rosa, standing and overlooking DC.

The wind picked up and so did the rustling noises. From our right, a particularly strong gust bent the wildly growing corn in a line heading toward our path, a line of dry stalks aimed directly at Celia.

From between the shifting yellow plants, I saw a brown blur. I froze.

"No!" I shouted, disbelieving.

Celia turned to see what was the matter.

Like a specter of death, Addy shot out of the corn and launched herself at Celia, who had turned just enough to spot the movement in her peripheral vision. The dog leapt with all the force of her weight behind her, slamming into Celia's midsection. The gun flew away as both dog and woman were propelled into the corn on the left of the path, out of view from where I stood. I raced up, noisily jangling the pack of supplies on my back as I ran.

I saw Addy, the dog we both loved, standing over Celia. Celia screamed as Addy bit into the flesh of her upper leg, making a terrible gaping wound. The dog was vicious and wild, its brown fur matted, wet-looking.

I stood stunned. My world spun. My friend. My *friends*. This couldn't be happening.

Celia screamed again, rolling away from the dog. Addy shook violently, spittle and blood flying, speckling the dry yellow corn stalks. Then the dog turned toward me.

For what seemed like forever, she simply stared. Then, emitting a low, gurgling growl, she approached.

"No, Addy, no," I pleaded, hands up before me. "Please. Stop. Please." Still she crept forward, looking at me with milky, seeping eyes.

I stepped backward and nearly tripped on something. The shotgun.

"Addy, please," I said, knowing it was pointless. Addy, my dog, was gone, replaced by this monster. A portion of my heart froze solid as I decided to act.

I wheeled and grabbed the gun. Addy took two steps and sprang at me, but even as she did, I spun the barrel toward her and fired.

My friend, my innocent, lovable friend, fell dead in a gasping lump, riddled with pellets from the gun. I sat gaping as she took her last breath. She looked up at me, not for an apology, not for pity, not with anger or mindless rage. In those last seconds, her eyes seemed to regain some of the warmth of life, just as that life was leaving her.

* * *

Hands shaking, I dropped the gun. I imagine it stayed right there until some other lost soul stumbled across it, who knows when later. All I knew was that I never wanted to touch it again.

I crawled over and put a hand on Addy. She didn't move. I wept as I stroked the bloody fur of her shoulder.

Off to the side among the corn, I heard a moan. Celia.

I jumped up, grabbed my pack, ran to her.

She was on her side, laying among the broken corn stalks with blood splashed and splattered all around her. I could see right away that she was in very bad shape. Her breathing was shallow and weak. I had to struggle to find a pulse. She barely opened her eyes to look up at me, then drifted back into unconsciousness. She was pale. Very pale.

Looking at the blood loss, I knew this was hypovolemic shock, and she would die, *soon*. Maybe in a hospital or even in my old office, I could save her, but we were in a damn cornfield. My will gave out and I flopped down, sitting beside Celia as her lifeblood escaped. I pounded the dirt with a balled fist. The wound on her leg was infused with dark blood and saliva. The metallic smell of blood filled my lungs.

I was sure that Addy had been infected by a zombie. And that meant...

Celia was now infected, too. Even if she didn't die here and now, she was dead. Rosa's cures, those eggs, weren't around to save her. I had nothing.

I sat with my arms wrapped around my knees, my head hanging low, as Celia's whispering breath went in and out.

Damn it. I felt so useless, doing nothing as my one friend lay dying, my other friend dead by my own hand just feet away. What a twisted triangle we'd become. Celia moaned slightly, her one hand shivering.

I lifted my head. I was *not* going to let Celia just die. I had to try something.

I rummaged through the supply pack until I found just what I wanted: the curved needle and some of the stronger thread. I pulled those out, along with a t-shirt and a tall plastic bottle containing our remaining water. I scurried over next to Celia.

First, I pulled off my belt and wrapped it around her upper thigh, tightening it to at least slow down the flow of blood. Then I used the water to rinse the wound. It was ragged, and any patch job I attempted would be difficult and heal poorly. That didn't matter, as long as it did heal. Even with the makeshift tourniquet, blood would seep again from the wound as soon as I rinsed it, so I pressed hard into the opening with the t-shirt. Then, to free my hands, I intertwined my legs around Celia's wounded leg, to hold the t-shirt in place and apply pressure. I pulled out the needle and thread.

Fumbling, hands shaking, I tried to thread the needle. I missed, over and over, eyes squinting at the tiny hole. Then, success. The thread went through. I held it and reached for the t-shirt, moving my body around for a better angle. That movement pulled the thread out, dropping it to the ground. I cursed at myself and twisted back. Again, I stabbed the thread at the needle, willing it to just *get the hell in the damn hole*. Finally, I got it.

This time, I held the threaded needle with a death grip, determined not to let it slip out again. I shifted my body and grabbed the t-shirt in one hand. It was getting soaked with Celia's blood, and her color was draining. How long did she have? I just acted on instinct, my training from younger days.

Jabbing the needle into her flesh, I made a series of haphazard stitches, a gross effort, just to pull the wound closed. Then, a quarter inch at a time, I made more precise stitches to pull her skin back together, down the length of the long gash. The end product was messy, like an intentionally grotesque scar for a Halloween costume. But the main bleeding seemed contained. The wound, however, still seeped blood. I had nothing left in the supply pack, so I simply improvised. I covered the sewn wound with the bloody t-shirt, wrapping leaves from the dried corn plants around the leg to tie it in place. I undid my belt tourniquet and moved it down to where it could hold the wound closed, tightening it enough to provide pressure but not cut off the blood flow. I took out a jacket and then stuffed the knapsack under her legs to prop them up. The jacket went on top of her as a blanket. Stepping back, I saw a ghost of Celia, a pale, deathly ill woman, lying in blood-soaked dirt, with the most laughably makeshift bandage ever made around her upper leg. But it would have to do.

To the south, in the far distance, the sound of people came again. The last sound I needed to hear.

I jumped up, ran to the top of the hill, scanned the surrounding land. To my left, not far off, a small barn with rotting, red-painted wood was standing. I charged over to it, into its shaded interior, looking wildly left and right. I found an old wheelbarrow covered in dirty cobwebs in one corner. Grabbing its handles, I pulled it down, turned back toward the door, and raced back to Celia.

Thankfully, Celia weighed much less than I did, but still I struggled. I tried to move her without tearing open the work I'd done on her leg, or even dislodging the ties of corn leaves holding things in place. I eventually got her into the wheelbarrow, head down in the metal body of the thing, legs angled upward toward the handles. I wanted to keep what little blood she had pooling near her head, in her brain. Sliding the pack onto my back again, I lifted the handles and began pushing north. The sounds of the approaching crowd increased to my south. I didn't dare turn around to look.

Stumbling down the path and over the hill, I pushed through the cornfield.

What was I doing? What was the point of all this? I didn't even know where I was going, just trying to get away. I'd left Addy, dead, behind me, and wheeled Celia, soon to be dead, in front of me. She was infected. This was pointless. Why was I doing it, still?

The whole world was a living hell. This whole world that kept tricking me into *trying*. Into *caring*. In the distance, maybe a mile to the north, I saw a small town. I headed there for no reason other than it was there and it was away from the mob to the south. Here I was, once again, trying to save someone, when I *knew* that saving people was impossible. Look at The Oasis. How many people had it saved, really, in the end? None. They all died. Look at Rosa. How many people had she saved? None. Not even herself.

Rosa: dead. Addy: dead. Harvey, Marian, Hank, Janine, the others: dead. And Celia. Even if I'd delayed her last breath for now, the disease had her. She was dead, too. Even I was dead, just a ragged old man shambling through fields, beyond salvation, the walking dead.

I let myself cry for all the lost ones, and for no reason at all, as I pushed the wheelbarrow toward a small road. Passing through the farmland, through the fields, I looked with wet, blurred vision at these hopeless pastures. There was no point to doing it, but I walked on.

Falling more than walking down the side of the small road toward the town, I nearly spilled Celia out of the wheelbarrow and into the rain-filled ditch that shadowed the road. My strength was leaving me rapidly.

I turned down one of the small streets lined with old shops that indicated the center of this little town. I vaguely scanned the front windows of the shops, thinking of finding shelter from the approaching mass of people.

I stopped.

There in front of me was an unexpected sight: a small medical clinic.

Its front door stood open, shadows hiding what was inside. I pulled the wheelbarrow up beside the door and left Celia there as I went in.

Everything was ransacked. I'd hoped to find medicine but there was nothing but smashed and empty bottles. I felt another wave of despair. Then I noticed that many of the clinic's other supplies remained. In addition to basic things like gauze and tape, there were blood-collection needles, drip tubes, clamps. Stuff that most people wouldn't know how to use. But I did.

In the back, I found several patient rooms. I chose the one that was the least cluttered, cleared off the exam table, and tried to make sure things looked as free from dirt as I could make them. It gave me visions of living in DC, keeping everything clean, holding off the tide of filth. But here, although I knew that I didn't want to risk additional infection, my ability to truly sterilize the room was nonexistent. I gathered supplies, organizing them on a wheeled U-base table and putting that next to the exam bed.

I went out to where Celia still lay upended in the wheelbarrow, feet up, head down. I tilted so that she was moved into a sort of standing position, then slid myself under and in front of her so she fell across my left shoulder. Hefting her up, I struggled into the clinic and managed to get her on the bed. She flopped down hard, but didn't budge, didn't make a sound. She was beyond pale, worse than even before, when I thought she might be dead. The t-shirt and corn leaves were soaked with blood. I had to work fast, but very carefully, doing something intricate that I'd never done before but only studied in basic theory, decades ago.

Bringing the rolling table along side, I reached for the water bottle and some gauze. I wet the gauze and cleaned her arm as best I could. There was nothing to truly sterilize her with, so this would have to do. I did the same to myself.

I gathered up two blood-collection sets and looked at them closely. They weren't meant to connect to each other, but I had to do it. On one, I uncapped the spike at the end of the drip tube. On the other, I removed the drip tube completely, carefully fitting the flexible PVC tubing over the spike of the other unit, making one long system, needle end connected to needle end. I was worried that it would become detached or that the spike would puncture the PVC, so I took the spike's cap and taped it to the connection point, like a splint for a broken bone, so it couldn't twist at that point. With more tape, I wrapped the connection, firm and complete, but not so thick and rigid that I wouldn't be able to get to a problem if one arose. Each kit had a rolling clamp on the PVC tubing; I closed both.

I knew my blood type was O negative, so a transfusion of red cells would be okay. But this would be a *whole*-blood transfusion, and anything could happen. Staring down at Celia's pale complexion and recognizing it as at least a Class III hemorrhage, possible Class IV, I had to do it. If she died, it was no different from what was already happening. And if for some reason I died… well, I think I'd seen enough for one lifetime.

My plan was to connect the flow of two bloodstreams together: anastomosis, it's called. Being right-handed, I put a rubber tourniquet on my left upper arm, and chose the most promising-looking vein near my left elbow. I shook my head in frustration, knowing that the simple act of inserting the line was something I could have offhandedly left to an assistant in my past life. I had to focus. I chose the median antebrachial and inserted the large bore needle delicately, remembering anatomy classes from so long ago, books and charts from my doctor days. I poked myself once, twice, three times, four. Sweat beaded on my brow. Looking over, I could barely see Celia's breathing, barely detect color in her skin. I tried to hit the vein again and failed. I was concerned that I'd have to try my right arm, complicating everything else I had to do, when the needle suddenly found the mark and blood flowed into the PVC tube, up to the rolling clamp. I taped the needle down, more than usual since I would be moving around, and sighed in relief. But I was hardly done.

Moving to Celia, I took the other side of my homemade transfusion kit and uncapped the needle. I took the tourniquet off me and put it on her upper arm, then I tapped her arm at the elbow to find the best vein. The median cubital seemed to be my best option, so I went for it. As I inserted the needle, her side of the PVC tubing also filled with blood up to the clamp. I'd have to remain standing, my arm higher than hers, to let gravity help the process. I returned the tourniquet to my arm, above the needle, so I could increase the pressure a bit more.

I rolled open the clamps, first on my side, then on hers, and watched the blood flow between us. I scanned her carefully for allergic reactions, but given her state, I probably could have been pouring arsenic into her veins with no visible effect.

I made my best guess on how to regulate the flow from me to her, trying not to overdo it but still working fast because of her condition. And then I was done. After the attack, the gunshot, triage in the field, the frantic flight that got us here, there was nothing to do but sit and wait.

Time passed.

A fatigue began to slowly, relentlessly seep into my bones. My eyelids slid down. I forced them back up. I tried to gauge the time, the flow, the amount of blood transferred, Celia's color. I had to stay on my feet.

Why was I doing this? She was still dead. The disease had her. I thought again about all the hard things, the horrific things, I had seen and done, all stemming from this one disease.

I closed my eyes and saw myself gun down Addy.

Time passed.

They say that time heals all wounds. I didn't believe that. Time *inflicted* wounds, one after the other, some small, some big, until finally you could no longer endure. You died. Time was not the healer of all. It was the destroyer.

Time passed.

I could barely stay awake. My knees trembled, buckled. I stumbled beside the bed, dangerously yanking the connected tubing between us.

One last thing…

I have…

To do…

I rolled the clamps closed and fell to the floor unconscious.

24

White.

Everything was blindingly white.

Was this death?

The barest of shadows passed in front of me, a form. A human form. A woman.

Rosa.

And then she was gone. Again.

* * *

Singing. I heard singing.

I tried to open my eyes, but the blinding whiteness outside was even greater than the blinding whiteness inside.

The singing stopped. "You awake?" a voice asked softly.

Celia.

Squinting, I raised my hand to shield my eyes. Why was my hand so heavy? Where was I?

Looking around, I saw the bottom of the exam bed, the legs of the U-base table. I was still in the clinic, on the floor. But I could feel a wad of clothes behind my head, a thermal blanket over me. In a raspy, dry voice, I asked, "How long?"

Celia knelt down beside me. "All told, I don't know. Because I don't know how long I was out. But it's been over a day since I woke up."

Over a day. Based on what I remembered of her condition, she would've been out for a while. It could have been as much as three days, total.

"I woke up *dying* of thirst," she said. "I drank what I could find, then got some of the last food from our bag over there." She pointed to it. "I figured you'd be really thirsty, too, so I put tiny capfuls of water in your mouth now and then. You sputtered them out pretty good a couple of times."

I suddenly realized how thirsty I was. Looking around, I saw Celia had a partial plastic bottle of water. I motioned toward it and she brought it to me. Drinking was hard, my throat uncooperative. But it was heaven.

She looked me in the eyes. "You saved my life. Thank you."

Returning the look, I had a moment of joy. Yes. She was *alive*.

But wait. What about…?

"How do you feel?" I asked, looking at her sideways.

Celia shrugged. "Fine, all things considered. My leg is a wreck, really hurts, and the stitches *itch*, I've got a headache, still weak, some other minor stuff, but you know… I'm okay."

"Fever?" I asked.

"I don't think so."

"What about any other symptoms? Lesions, lack of feeling on your hands or face, any delusions or fits of anger?" As I sat up, she pushed back, understanding my point.

"Wait, you think I'm...?" She couldn't say it. *Infected.*

I paused, trying to break it to her gently. "The dog. Addy was sick. Infected. The disease — RL2013 — I'm sure she had it."

"But I don't feel infected, not with... *it*... Not like I've heard about it."

I thought about it. Three days, as an estimate. And she didn't look infected. I reached out and touched her cheek, her fingertips. "Feel normal?"

"Yeah."

"Well, I agree. Normal skin." I sat and thought some more.

The blood. The *whole* blood. The red cells. The platelets. And the white blood cells.

Unlike during a normal blood transfusion, I hadn't separated my blood out, filtered it, radiated it. I hadn't done anything but put my blood — my whole, *cured* blood — into her body. My eyebrows raised.

She noticed. "What is it?" She was nervous about what I was saying.

"Maybe — just *maybe*," I held up one finger in a cautioning pose, "my blood passed something along to you during the transfusion. Antibodies. A resistance."

"You mean… the *cure?*" She said it quietly, like she was afraid the idea would run away from her if she was too loud.

"Yeah." I grinned. "That's what I mean."

A dawning smile broke across her face. "You're not kidding with me, are you?" She was beginning to bubble up, excitedly.

"I wouldn't kid about that," I said.

She flung herself at me, hugging me. She laughed, and I had to join her.

There we sat, on the floor of an abandoned clinic, in some small, desolate town on the Eastern Shore of Maryland, laughing like hyenas, hugging, rocking back and forth. We must have made a hell of an unexpected racket.

I started to cry. The first tears of joy I could recall in who knows how long. The blood. *My* blood. I truly believed it had cured Celia. And if that was the case, things had changed. They had changed beyond my wildest imagination. There was a new cure, and it was me.

After plodding along for so long, finding something then watching it stripped away, thinking there was nothing at all left for me to live for, now I suddenly had this: *I needed to live, so that others could, too.*

Then suddenly from outside the room, there was a voice.

"Hello…?" a woman said, tentatively.

We froze, holding our breath.

"Hello? Is someone back there?" the woman asked.

I looked at Celia, and our eyes met. Looking around the tiny, enclosed exam room, it was clear. There was no hiding this time. No escape. I nodded to her, and she pushed away and up. I stood, gingerly. She followed me to the door of the exam room.

I turned toward the front of the clinic, toward the waiting room, and there stood a middle-aged woman with brown disheveled hair, her white blouse and jeans splotched with dirt, a pistol strapped to her side. Behind her, people crowded all around the waiting room. Men — old, young, some of them also carrying guns — women, even a child or two. Their numbers led back out the open door to the street, where I could see dozens more standing in the sunlight, all looking toward us. A few of them looked concerned, or surprised, but mostly they were tired, spent.

Celia and I stepped into the hall and the woman in front pulled her hand up to the pistol at her side. I raised one hand, palm outward facing her.

"Hi," I said.

THE END

The story concludes with

From Blood Reborn — The Oasis of Filth — Part 3

Thank you so much for reading my book! Here's a little bit about me, Keith Soares. I live in Alexandria, Virginia, with my wife and two daughters. By day, my wife and I run a web, mobile and app development studio, which means that writing is my second job. Creativity has always been a huge focus for me, whether making music, coding video games, drawing or writing. *The Oasis of Filth* is my first published novel.

Visit my website at **http://keithsoares.com** for information on other books and upcoming projects. While you're there, I hope you consider joining my mailing list where I can keep you updated on future books.

www.ingramcontent.com/pod-product-compliance
Lightning Source LLC
Chambersburg PA
CBHW021104130626
46554CB00002B/525